"I'm here to rescue you."

His hands were tightly closed around her wrists, where they would remain until he was confident that she wasn't going to take a swing at him.

For a moment, still sprawled on top of him, Pru wavered. She was being rescued? And then suspicion crept in between the lines. "Where are the others?"

"There are no others," Joshua told her.

Her eyes widened. "You're it?"

"Yup. Lucky me. Not that I wouldn't find this position interesting at any other time." He opened his hands, releasing her wrists. "But I think we'd better get out of here before one of those Neanderthals comes to investigate."

Pru scrambled to her feet, managing to have more than just marginal contact with all parts of him. "Just who the hell are you?" she demanded hotly, her cheeks burning.

A smile twisted his lips. "At the moment, your savior."

Dear Reader,

I don't know about you, but my favorite stories revolve around the irresistible force meeting the immovable object: two equally stubborn, independent people who discover that there is no weakness to letting another person into their worlds. In this case, the prime minister's daughter, known in the tabloids as "Pru the Shrew," has met her match in Joshua, the hunky special agent who has been sent to rescue her from her kidnappers. I knew there were going to be fireworks before I ever started writing about them.

This book marks the beginning of a miniseries involving the organization that was first introduced in the CAPTURING THE CROWN series. The Lazlo Group is a highly secretive, extremely efficient organization of handpicked operatives who always get the job done, no matter what it might be. I had a ball writing this, and I hope you have as much fun reading it.

As always, I thank you for reading and I wish you love,

Marie Ferrarella

MARIE FERRARELLA

My Spy

Silhouette®

Romantic

SUSPENSE

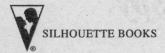

SILHOUETTE BOOKS

ISBN-13: 978-0-373-27542-7
ISBN-10:   0-373-27542-0

MY SPY

Books by Marie Ferrarella

Silhouette Romantic Suspense

*Cavanaugh Justice
**The Doctors Pulaski

MARIE FERRARELLA

This *USA TODAY* bestselling and RITA® Award-winning author has written over one hundred and fifty books for Silhouette, some under the name Marie Nicole. Her romances are beloved by fans worldwide. Check out her Web site at www.MarieFerrarella.com.

To Jenny and John Cho. If you love each other, all the rest will work itself out. Have a wonderful life!

Chapter 1

The silence in his bedroom was eerie, enveloping him like a black embrace. He sat there for a moment, listening to the sound of his own heartbeat. The sound of his own breathing.

It wasn't often that he woke up in the middle of the night in a cold sweat. Sweat was for people who had things to lose. Home, family, possessions they treasured, a reputation they couldn't rebuild. But Corbett Lazlo had long since left all of that behind.

There were no ties.

In general, he spent most of his time in the offices of the organization he had created fourteen years ago and presided over like a benevolent god. For the most part, although there were flesh-and-blood people who shared his last name, his organization was his family, his child.

But even that, although he took pride in it, was expendable.

Long ago he'd learned that nothing was permanent, that no one thing could actually be thought of as his lifeline to the world. He did not allow himself to indulge in the emotions that both plagued and regaled other men. Emotions, he firmly believed, more often than not could spell a man's downfall.

The way his had almost destroyed him.

It was a dream of Cassandra that had him bolting upright in his solitary bed, perspiring when the temperature in his current Paris apartment was kept a constant sixty-seven degrees. Not really a dream, more like a fragment of a memory, delivered to him across the rough sea of time. Cassandra, beckoning to him, devouring him. Honey-haired, green-eyed Cassandra, as young, as beautiful, as seductive as the first moment he laid eyes on her.

And just as evil.

There'd been a glint in her eyes, a murderous glint just as her embrace tightened, a fraction of a second before her mouth came down on his, that warned him of what was to come.

Of death if he didn't flee.

Corbett sat up in his bed for a moment, his black

silk sheets cool against his hot skin. He dragged a hand through his silver hair, slowly drawing air back into his lungs.

The memory…a warning?

A premonition?

He had not remained alive in this precarious, constant high-stakes, cat-and-mouse existence by ignoring his gut instinct. Just because he'd been asleep was no reason to doubt that something was reaching out to him, trying to warn him.

But about what?

Cassandra DuMont was long in his past. The daughter of a cold-blooded, heartless man, Maximilian DuMont, who had been the head of an organization that went to the highest bidder, no task too loathsome, no moral line left uncrossed. The agents at MI-6 had referred to it as Snake, but that was an inside joke. The organization had no name. It was evil, undefined.

There'd been a brother, too. Apollo. Groomed to take over his father's place when the time came. Dead by *his* hand, Corbett thought. Cassandra hadn't known that when she'd made love with him. If she had, she would have tried to slit his throat. And he would have been forced to slit hers.

Instead of sparing her the way he had.

He'd been soft then. And naive. Believing in justice, truth and all the hype he'd been sold when he was first inducted into Britain's Secret Intelligence Service—S.I.S., formerly MI-6. He and his comrades were protectors of the realm. He'd believed that they would stand by him and he by them.

Until the allegations came.

And then, suddenly, he was alone. Watching his entire world, his carefully crafted career, crash and burn. They'd called him a double agent and said they had the evidence to prove it.

The stillness continued.

Corbett took a long breath, as if the air in his lungs would place that period of time even further from him than the actual years did.

Before he could mount a defense, he was swiftly brought up on charges of treason and convicted on the basis of fabricated evidence. His father, a former Hungarian refugee who'd risen to some prominence in Parliament, turned from him, calling him a disgrace even though the old man had never wanted him to be part of S.I.S. in the first place. The words that cut deepest were the ones he'd heard from his mother, saying she was ashamed of him.

And then, out of the blue, Edward, his womanizing older brother, came to his rescue, providing money that allowed Adam Sinclair, Corbett's best friend and right-hand man, to bribe enough guards to bring about Corbett's escape from prison. There was no love lost between the brothers, but Edward said he knew Corbett to be a loyal man and loyal men did not sell out their country.

The words, more than the money, forever placed him in Edward's debt. And, somewhat ironically,

Edward had become the financial handler for the Lazlo Group.

With Adam, Corbett had fled the country, coming to France. When he'd created the Lazlo Group, Adam was the first agent he recruited to join. Together, they oversaw the labor pains of its concrete formation. But if asked, Adam always gave him the credit for the group's inception. It was the Lazlo Group, not the Lazlo–Sinclair Group.

Originally, the agency had been created as a means to prove Corbett's innocence. His intention was to discover who had planted all the damning evidence against him. But even now, more than a decade later, he still had no answers.

He had, however, managed—thanks to the advances in forensic science and the introduction of DNA as a tool—to prove that he had never betrayed his country.

Apologies were issued. The S.I.S., saying all was forgiven, wanted him back. But he hadn't wanted it back. Because all was not forgiven, as far as he was concerned.

These days, he had little time to pursue a trail that was close to seventeen years cold. The Lazlo Group had grown from two to more than fifty. It was now an international team of highly trained agents with a myriad of talents and skills, not the least of which was discretion. Corbett's nephew, Edward's son Joshua, had surprised Corbett by becoming one of his best agents.

The Group was also perhaps the best-kept secret in the free world among the upper rungs of governments. Usually called in as a last resort, or when a situation was of such a delicate, discreet nature that no one else could be trusted to handle it, the ever-growing organization had more work than it knew what to do with. Consequently, there was no time to investigate a personal wrong done to him so many years ago.

But he would eventually solve the puzzle, Corbett promised himself. He didn't believe in loose ends.

Corbett had no idea how long he'd been in his office at the high-tech yet largely inconspicuous Lazlo Group headquarters before he heard the low, melodic sound that indicated he'd received another missive on his computer.

He swung his swivel chair around to face the state-of-the-art machine that Lucia, his wizard of all things computer, had insisted he get, and looked at the flat panel screen.

There was a single sentence on it.

The day of repentance draws near, Lazlo.

The moment he read it, his phone rang. Only a handful of his operatives and a select few heads of state had the direct number to his office. In the case of the latter, the signal was bounced and rerouted to several terminals throughout the world before it finally reached him. Just another device to protect his whereabouts and his people. Trust No One was more than just a once-popular cult saying. It was a credo that kept him alive and strong.

Picking up the receiver, he said, "Lazlo," in a calm, resonant voice. The same voice that had soothed distraught world leaders when they were confronted with the kidnapping of a loved one. The same voice that promised secrecy and a swift resolution above all else.

There was no hint of the disquiet that currently resided beneath his reserve.

"It's Henderson."

After Sinclair, Wallace Henderson was the group's oldest operative. Even more than Sinclair, Henderson prided himself on remaining unruffled. But Corbett's trained ear detected a strain in the other man's voice.

He wasn't wrong. After a beat, Henderson said, "Lazlo, someone killed Jane Kiley."

The already military straight posture stiffened even more. Corbett's hand tightened on the receiver. His words of praise were few and he showed no signs of making emotional connections, but that didn't change the fact that he was very protective of his people.

"When?" he demanded. "How?"

Henderson recited the bare bones. "An hour ago. Lisbon. Car bomb."

Henderson's voice cracked. It wasn't the result of one agent's indignation over another's murder. Corbett knew about his people, knew without being directly informed by the parties involved that Henderson and Kiley had been lovers ever since they'd been partnered on a case a little more than a year ago. They probably thought they were being discreet enough to avoid detection. But few things escaped Corbett's notice.

"Do we know who?" he asked, already making notes to himself. When it came to keeping track of events, he reverted to paper and pencil. The old way. But this time around, he also didn't want to use the computer any more than he had to until Lucia took a look at it. There had to be a way to trace the sender of the message.

"No." Henderson ground out the word, frustration echoing in his voice. "She'd just wrapped up the case you sent her on. The munitions were safely returned to their original owner, as per instruction. She'd had the money wired to the Swiss account and verified the transaction." One tiny, shaky breath escaped before Henderson regained control. "She was coming home."

"Find the son of a bitch who did this," Corbett ordered. There was no emotion in his voice, only volume, but his people understood that was his way of coping. "And bring her back," he added more quietly.

"But—"

He heard the bewilderment in Henderson's voice. They both knew what the end result of a car bombing looked like. A charred body at best, a disintegrated one at worst.

"Whatever you can find, Henderson," Corbett told him, his voice less gruff despite the fact that he was having a difficult time coping with this news. They'd lost only one man on the job since the group came into being. Nathaniel O'Hara had been a demolitions expert trying to disarm a bomb strapped to a man's chest. Neither the man nor O'Hara made it out of that afternoon alive. But the bomber had been brought down a week later. Corbett had been in on the kill. "I'm sending Taggert to go over the scene."

He ended the call before Henderson could say anything more. The next moment, he called Taggert with instructions to take the first flight to Lisbon.

After that, he sent for Lucia. He wanted to know where the message on his screen had come from.

The perspiration forming along his hairline did not go unnoticed. There had to be a tie-in between what had happened to Kiley, the message on his screen and his nightmare. He didn't believe in coincidences, not even when they involved dreams.

Most of the time, Prudence Hill, daughter of the prime minister of England, liked to shake things up. By definition, she was not a creature of habit. However, some things in her life just naturally seemed to fall into a pattern. Barring a monsoon or a pronounced case of the flu, she always jogged first thing in the morning. And her route was always the same.

Unencumbered by bodyguards, which she vehemently refused to live with, she ran clockwise along the oblong perimeter of St. James Park until it eventually fed back to the street she started out on, at which point she'd jog back to her apartment. It was as close to a country setting as she could get in the West End.

Pru preferred running as early as possible, when there were fewer cars out. She was more than a little aware of the irony of attempting to maintain a healthy cardiovascular regimen while breathing in the exhaust fumes being belched out by the many vehicles that sped or crawled along the London streets. But it couldn't be helped. Since breathing in exhaust was a permanent part of the equation in London whether or not she jogged, she chose to jog.

Perspiration slid down her spine, working its way through her sports bra and turning her baggy T-shirt into an uncomfortable collection of cotton threads that adhered to her body. The air was heavy. The famous runner's high had found her less than midway through her jog, but it was battling mightily with fatigue because the weather was so oppressive.

Jogging in place, waiting for the light to turn green so she could cross, Pru slipped into her own world. The sense of euphoria she was trying to maintain blended well with the music she was listening to. Consequently, she took no notice of the white van that abruptly stopped less than a foot away from her, didn't hear the passenger side doors opening and didn't see the two men dressed in black jerseys, black slacks and ski masks who swiftly leaped out of the vehicle.

Eyes intent on the traffic signal, Pru was completely unaware of the men until the two grabbed her, one from the side, the other from behind, and attempted to drag her into the van.

Startled, Pru reacted instantly. Twisting, she bit the hand that was covering her mouth.

The assailant who was behind her and whose fleshy palm now had an almost perfect impression of her teeth howled in pain. He jerked his hand back, uncovering her mouth.

"She bit me!" he cried, furious. "The damn bitch bit me!"

"Suck it up," the man to his right snapped.

Pru's semi-freedom lasted less than half a heartbeat as the other man's grasp on her tightened. Though she twisted and bucked, it was useless. Within thirty seconds of the initial encounter, she'd been packed away in the rear of the van like baggage. Even before the doors were shut, the vehicle was whisking away in the opposite direction of her apartment.

The only minor triumph she'd attained, other than leaving her mark on the tallest of the three kidnappers, was that she'd managed to drop her MP3 player where they'd grabbed her. It was the only clue she could leave. The player, a gift from her stepmother, had her initials on it.

Now all that had to happen was for the device to remain unnoticed until someone her father sent came along to retrace her steps.

She tried not to think of the odds.

"What do you want?" she demanded, seething.

She was being manhandled and for two cents, given half an opportunity, she would have cut the hearts out of all three of their chests. Her hands were already bound behind her and one of the three men was crouching in front of her, wrapping duct tape around her ankles. She felt like a damned Christmas turkey about to be shoved into the oven.

"For you to shut up!" the assailant she'd bitten snapped.

Before she could retort, the man who'd been binding her feet rose to his knees and pressed a length of gray, sticky duct tape across her mouth. "That should do it," the man told his companion proudly as he began to rise to his feet.

Before he could, Pru threw her weight forward as she jerked her head down, hitting her forehead against his with all the force she could muster. It was enough to catch him off guard and send him staggering backward. He fell on his butt as he cried out in pain, then began to curse. A hail of expletives rained down on her.

And then a sudden, searing pain exploded not from the initial point of contact on her forehead, but from the back of her skull.

The world went black before she could struggle to hold the smothering blanket at bay.

The last thought Pru had was that she was dead.

Chapter 2

When he wasn't working, Joshua Lazlo found himself at loose ends. While his professional life was precision personified, his private life was the exact opposite.

He had no doubt that if his uncle Corbett had not plucked him out of the social whirl he had resided in from the tender age of sixteen, making a tentative offer to him to join his "group," his life would have been a complete and utter shamble. More than likely, he would be well on his way to becoming this generation's version of his father. Which probably would have been more than his poor mother, Abigail, could stand.

Ambitious, his father, Edward Lazlo, had made a

small name for himself in Parliament over the years. He'd made a bigger name for himself among the ladies. A scandalous womanizer, he never allowed the fact that he was married to interfere with his actual life's ambition: to bed as many women as humanly possible before he died.

Not that there was anything wrong with that, Joshua thought, a half smile playing on his lips as he made his way into the bathroom. Though not exactly an admirable avocation, it did have its merits.

There were, after all, a great many beautiful women in the world.

But the fact that these affairs, after all this time, still bothered his poor mother, despite her rather sad little charade that she was unaware of her husband's philandering, bothered him in turn. There was no love lost between his father and him.

A man shouldn't marry if he had no intention of remaining faithful.

Which was why, Joshua reasoned, not for the first time as he stepped into the sleek, black onyx tiled shower stall, he was never going to get married. The world was filled with an endless supply of delightful women with long limbs, soft curves and willing bodies.

And he'd never met one he wanted to spend more than a weekend with.

Joshua turned on the water, moving the lever toward the hot side. It was his day off, but there was no reason to spend it with the scent of Miranda still clinging to his body.

Not unless Miranda was close at hand, he added silently.

When he was on assignment, he could work round the clock. Adrenaline pounding, he needed little to no sleep to keep him going. But on his days off, he changed completely, sleeping in, allowing the sun to rise without him.

He supposed it could be called recharging his batteries. Or viewed as being the sloth he could so easily revert to had his uncle not seen something in him and turned him into a crusader.

Not that they were associated with any specific higher power or world government. The agents who comprised the Lazlo Group were essentially free-lancers. It gave his uncle the privilege of being able to turn down whatever work he didn't choose to do.

When all was said and done, the causes they took up, the people they aided, could all be found on the side of freedom and democracy.

With the possible exception of the time eighteen months ago when he'd had to save the wife and son of the Chinese ambassador from a radical fringe group of would-be terrorists. It had been touch and go for a harrowing thirty-six hours before he brought them both to safety. Since then an expensive bottle of vintage wine had arrived at his door the first of every month like clockwork.

He liked to think that he had accomplished a bit of détente in rescuing the ambassador's family. Not to mention sending up the price of vintage wine.

"Maybe you're not as worthless as the old man says you are," he murmured under his breath, sticking his head under the steady stream of water and removing the shampoo from his hair.

The old man, of course, was his father, who had never had a good word to say to him from the time when such things had actually mattered. Now, all his father's disdain meant to Joshua was that he was doing something right with his life. He knew that his father found it particularly galling that he was working with his uncle and that he quietly admired the man. There was no denying that Edward Lazlo was a jealous man, jealous of any attention not sent directly his way.

The pulsating noise slowly wove its way through the sound of the shower's running water.

Joshua stopped, listening. Shutting off the water, he angled his head to hear better.

Ringing.

It was his cell phone.

The next second, Joshua swiftly left the confines of his shower, marking his path with splotches of water that dripped off his body as he retrieved his phone from the nightstand where he'd left it. Day off or not, he knew better than to ignore the phone when it rang.

He'd had the presence of mind, just before falling into bed last night, to plug the phone in. It was still tethered to his charger.

Joshua didn't bother disconnecting the device as he picked it up. Flipping the phone open, he pressed it to his ear.

"Lazlo."

"Where are you?"

The sound of his uncle's voice took him aback for a second. Ordinarily, the man had one of his people do his calling.

Joshua disconnected the phone from its charger and walked back into the bathroom.

"My place." Taking a towel from the rack, he began drying himself with one hand. He had a feeling he wasn't going to be climbing back into the shower. "It's my day off," he added needlessly. His uncle was on top of everything that happened or didn't happen at the agency, but it didn't hurt to add that little fact in.

"Not anymore."

The finality of the tone was familiar. Something was up. His uncle didn't pull strings just to watch people jump.

"I'm listening."

"If you weren't, you wouldn't be working for me," Corbett replied crisply. "The British prime minister's daughter is missing. She was apparently kidnapped sometime this morning."

"Why?"

The question was a spontaneous response to the information. He could think of a lot of other people who would have been easier to kidnap than Prudence Hill. The kidnappers obviously hadn't realized what they were in for when they took the young woman. The tabloids, who loved to hound people of prominence, to build up and then tear down the same person within the space of a few paragraphs, had dubbed Prime Minister Jeremy Hill's older daughter "Pru the Shrew."

According to so-called "friends"—most likely disgruntled hangers-on that she'd had no patience with—Prudence Hill had a waspish disposition and never minced words. Word, among people who supposedly would know about such things, had it that the diplomatic corps would not be calling the prime minister's daughter any time soon with an invitation to join their ranks.

"You'll be briefed when you arrive." Joshua knew that his uncle didn't believe in saying any more than absolutely necessary over the telephone, even if the lines were secured and tested on a daily basis. "The rest you will find out and cover in the report that you will give to me after you bring the young woman back."

Complete faith, that was what he liked about his uncle. The man did not waste words, did not heap accolades of any kind for a job well done. Nonetheless, you knew what he thought, knew where you stood with him. In Corbett Lazlo's case, a simple nod spoke volumes and was all but euphoric for the recipient.

"Yes, sir," Joshua responded. He finished drying himself and draped the towel haphazardly over the rack then padded back to his bedroom. Time was ticking away.

"There's a jet waiting for you at the airport. Be there in forty minutes. Murphy is compiling a dossier on the woman for you. It'll be waiting for you when you get to the airfield." There was an infinitesimal pause. "I don't have to tell you to be discreet."

"No," Joshua agreed amicably, opening his closet, "you don't."

He knew the rules. He was to get in and out without leaving a mark, retrieve the girl and bring her home—alive—as swiftly as possible. To aid him he had complete access to all the latest electronic gadgets and available technology, not to mention the considerable standard resources of the Lazlo Group, both human and otherwise, the caliber of which would have made James Bond salivate had the character actually existed.

In exchange for the faith placed in him and the arsenal at his disposal, he could never protest that an assignment found him at an inconvenient moment, nor that he might need more than the allotted amount of time to arrive at the appointed place. Corbett expected loyalty, compliance and agents who were as close to perfection as humanly possible. For this he paid extremely well. But there were rewards beyond money to garner.

He was just now beginning to find that out, Joshua thought, taking out a casual pair of cream-colored slacks and a navy jacket. A light blue shirt followed, along with whisper small briefs and dark, thin socks. All his clothes were aerodynamically light. You never knew when you had to flee and maximum speed was always good if your vehicle was "accidentally" destroyed.

The satisfaction of a job well done was nothing compared to the slight glimmer of approval occasionally seen in Corbett Lazlo's eyes. And because he'd found himself such a student of his uncle, Joshua had become acutely attuned to the various nuances in the older man's voice.

There was something more there now, something that Corbett Lazlo was not saying. Had he been the perfect agent, he would have refrained from asking. But Joshua had not yet completely morphed into a junior version of his uncle and so allowed himself to press the issue a little.

"Is something wrong, Uncle?"

He heard annoyance when his uncle answered. "Other than the fact that the older daughter of one of the most influential men in the entire free world has been kidnapped?"

His uncle made it sound as if that was more than enough reason for him to be troubled and distracted, but Joshua knew better. Very little ruffled Corbett Lazlo and they were in the business of thwarting international kidnappers among other things. There was something more, he'd bet his life on it.

"Other than the fact that the older daughter of one of the most influential men in the entire free world has been kidnapped," Joshua parroted back, then waited to be filled in.

The pause on the other end of the line made him uneasy. It stretched out until it was as thin as a piano wire.

The feeling did not leave once his uncle began speaking again.

"Jane Kiley's dead."

He knew Jane. A small, thin woman with lightning-fast hands, a sharp mind and a smile that rivaled a sunrise. She knew her way around horses and tanks, an odd combination that came in handy. He felt an instant sense of loss. He also sensed that there was more.

"I'm guessing not from natural causes." It was said for form's sake. They wouldn't be talking about it if the causes had been natural.

"There was a car bomb."

Joshua could feel his gut tightening in sympathetic response. "Part of the case?"

"The case was closed," Corbett said flatly.

Joshua could hear his uncle weighing his words in the silence that followed. Corbett was known to be closemouthed about almost everything. Information—*any* information—was released on a need-to-know basis. Even about something like this. Joshua didn't have to be told that Corbett already had the right people working on this.

"Be careful, Joshua."

The warning took him aback. That was a first,

Joshua thought. His uncle never troubled himself with the risk factors. An assignment was gone over, assessed, then left up to the chosen agent to successfully execute. No mention was ever made of being careful.

Until now.

This was serious, Joshua thought to himself. Really serious.

"Not to worry," Joshua told him buoyantly. "Today is *not* a good day to die," he said, paraphrasing an ancient Cheyenne saying. "I'm on my way."

"Of course you are."

The connection terminated after Corbett's last uttered syllable. Joshua was on his own.

He hurried into his clothes, into his holster and weapon and out the front door as if the devil was after him.

Because he very well might be.

Forty minutes later found Joshua Lazlo sprinting across the private airfield to one of his uncle's private jets. The moment the pilot saw him approaching, he began to go through the necessary checklist, the end of which would allow him to take to the air. They had only a short transatlantic hop ahead of them, since the first destination would be London. He was to meet with the prime minister and the man's chief advisor and oldest friend, George Montgomery, to personally obtain all the information that was available.

Clarence Murphy stood just within the plane's entrance, waiting as Joshua took the steps up to the plane two at a time. The carryall that he kept perpetually packed and ready to go in his closet was slung over his shoulder.

Taking the carryall from him, Murphy stepped back, waited until he was on board and then closed and latched the door.

"No need to get a stitch from running," Murphy told him. He gestured toward a seat, then took the one opposite it, buckling up. "It's not like we can leave without you, seeing as you're the reason for this quick hop."

The dossier that Corbett had promised was on the seat, waiting for him. Joshua picked it up before sitting down. Buckled into his seat, he crossed his leg over his thigh and rested the folder on it.

"No," Joshua contradicted as he opened up the dossier and scanned the pages within the black folder. There was a wealth of information waiting for him, all neatly cataloged and arranged by year. "The prime minister's daughter is."

Chapter 3

The first thing he noticed was how vivid her hair was, even through a telescope at this distance.

Joshua wiped away another large, fat raindrop that seemed to fall on him in slow motion, and refocused on his target. Prudence Hill was a redhead and the tabloids really must have had it in for her, he thought, trying to ignore the pregnant promise of a downpour. He gazed intently into the back window of the run-down farmhouse from his vantage point some one hundred yards away.

The pictures he'd seen on the covers of the same rags that had given her infamy of a sort made her look austere, frightening, with definite wicked-witch-of-the-west attributes. The headlines screamed as much, as did the nickname the magazines had all summarily bestowed on her: Pru the Shrew.

But if the woman he was looking at actually was the British prime minister's headstrong, outspoken daughter, then somewhere along the line, someone had made a big mistake. Not only that, but someone definitely needed to spring for better cameras for their photographers, because the only resemblance the gagged, bound young woman in the cluttered back bedroom of the isolated, dilapidated building had to the woman in the tabloid photographs that had been taken was that they both had red hair.

Beyond that, the difference between the two was like that between a butterfly and a moth. They both had wings and they both flew, but one was beautiful and graceful while the other plain and shunned. The woman he'd sometimes seen portrayed on the tabloid covers beneath unflattering adjectives had dull, lifeless hair, dowdy clothing and a body that wouldn't give a person the slightest pause or merit even a first glance, much less a second. That wasn't true of the woman in the white jogging shorts and baggy but clingy T-shirt. And from what he could see, she had unconditionally killer legs.

Her profile was to him and, despite the duct tape, he could see that her face, though flushed, was more than passingly attractive. He couldn't see her eyes, which to him had always been one of the most important weapons in a woman's arsenal, but he suspected that there was fire in them.

Which would make her beautiful, not school-marmish. The tabloids loved her for her sensational comments and hated her for her attitude toward them, which was pure contempt. As to the discrepancy in appearance, he had a feeling that whoever was in charge of reviewing the final copy probably did what had been covertly done in the past: taken her head and pasted it onto someone else's body, making sure they used the most unflattering photo of Prudence they could find.

If he'd been armed with nothing more than their photos, he'd never have found her.

But it had taken more than just flashing around her photograph, obtained from the prime minister's assistant, to locate the missing young woman. It had taken the combined backing of a crack team in Paris, Lucia with her almost magical capabilities with the computer, and luck.

He never underestimated the power of luck. Because luck had Mr. Merriweather Wilson walking up to the guard at 10 Downing Street ten minutes after he, Joshua, had been ushered into the prime minister's presence. Wilson, he was told, began innocently enough by saying that he had something he believed belonged to the prime minister's older daughter.

The moment the words were out of his mouth, Wilson had instantly been taken into a basement room within the historical residence and thoroughly, repeatedly, questioned.

The prime minister's people had thought, at first, that Wilson was part of the kidnapping plot, sent to up the ante that had initially been set. But the poor, clueless man protested over and over again that his son Derek had found the MP3 player that morning near the park. Intending to keep his newfound prize, Derek could have easily done so if Wilson had not been running late that morning, not having yet departed for his very important position at the West End Bank.

Wilson had actually been on his way out when he'd taken note of the MP3 player clipped like a newly captured trophy to his sixteen-year-old's belt. He stopped to question his son, who'd recently entered a rather shady period of his life. Thinking the player to be stolen, he'd been left unmoved by his son's impassioned protestations of innocence. But Derek remained steadfast, firmly maintaining that he had found the MP3 player, not stolen it from someone.

Employing as much drama as he could, Wilson told his former interrogators that his jaw had practically dropped to the floor when he read the inscription on the back of the player. He'd lost no time in bringing it to Number 10 because he was a patriot— and because, he added more quietly, he was hoping that there might be some small reward for the player's recovery.

Joshua had left that part up to the other men in the room, the prime minister's personal bodyguards and his best friend, Montgomery, a kindly faced man who towered over the others. Joshua remained focused. He'd asked Wilson exactly where the player had been located. Wilson had to defer to his son. The latter was summoned. Derek was quick to pick up that something had to be amiss and made an attempt to barter.

But there was to be no exchange of information, on that the prime minister was absolutely clear. No one, except a very select few, was to even know that his daughter was missing.

On that Joshua and the prime minister had been in agreement.

Taken to the exact spot where Derek Wilson had first been united with the MP3 player, Joshua had the prime minister's people fan out and locate every security camera in the area. After the London subway bombings of two years past, local small businesses, not to mention the government, had installed security cameras in as many available nooks and crannies as possible.

They got luckier. A grainy film of the abduction was recovered.

From that came a poor photograph of the van used and a much magnified partial license plate. Turning everything over to Lucia via the capabilities of his highly advanced cell phone, Joshua was rewarded in short order with the name of the van's owner.

The prime minister sent two of his people to the

owner's house. He wasn't there. But a hit on one of his credit cards at a distant gas station, also thanks to Lucia, showed them the path that the van had taken. Away from London and into the countryside, the land of the sisters Brontë, haystacks and needles. In other words, it appeared that they were headed north, in the general vicinity of Haworth.

It was an easy place to get lost. Or to hold a hostage.

Eager, distraught, the prime minister wanted to send some of his people along when he'd discovered that Joshua had come alone. But he'd respectfully declined the offer, saying he worked best on his own and unimpeded. If the cavalry was sent in, Prudence would be dead before they made it to the front door.

Reluctantly, the prime minister agreed to his terms.

Joshua continued tracking and following slim leads until, a day and a half after Prudence Hill had been snatched outside of the southern end of St. James Park, he had wound up here, in an isolated section of the countryside relatively untouched in the last 170 years, staring through a telescope at a filthy window into an even filthier room.

Staring directly at the object of his search.

She looked none the worse for her ordeal, Joshua judged, relieved that the young woman was still alive. Now all he had to do was to keep her that way, get her out of there in one piece and bring her back to her father.

A tall order from where he stood. But not an impossible one.

Joshua rose to his feet, reducing the telescope in his hands to a fraction of its original size. The fat drops of rain began to increase and fall in earnest. The sky had been an odd shade of amber and mauve all day and there'd been talk of an electrical storm on the horizon. He'd hoped that the weather would hold steady until he got Prudence out of there.

In true black ops tradition, Joshua began turning the situation around in his mind, searching for a way to make it work for him rather than against him.

Ten minutes later, his clothes sticking to his body and his hair plastered to his head, Joshua walked up to the kidnappers' front door and knocked urgently. All he knew was that the farmhouse, which belonged to one Owen Sutton now that his grandfather had passed on, contained anywhere from two to four people, not counting their hostage. No one knew what Owen's source of income was, since the farm was not a working one.

Joshua had a hunch he knew.

Hidden inside his left boot was an extra clip of bullets for the gun tucked into the back of his waistband.

He knocked again when there was no response.

It was several tense seconds before the door was finally opened. An average, unfriendly looking man of medium height and build, dressed completely in black, stood squarely in the doorway. There was a streak of what looked like pale pink face powder across the cuff of his left sleeve. From carrying Prudence, Joshua surmised, unless the man had some peculiar habits.

Eyes like cold, black marbles passed over him. "Yeah?"

Joshua looked properly humbled, a hapless man without a clue as to how to remedy the situation he found himself in.

"I'm sorry to bother you, mate, but my car broke down about a mile away—" he pointed vaguely toward the road "—and I was wondering if you'd mind my using your telephone."

The man in the doorway looked as if he would have rather shoved his face into the nearest deep puddle than to allow him access into the farmhouse. "What for?" he spat out.

Joshua shrugged helplessly. "To call a mechanic, a towing service, someone for help…" His voice trailed off.

The man eyed him for a long time. Joshua felt as if he were being X-rayed. Obviously coming to no conclusion, the man lifted his chin pugnaciously. "How come you ain't got a cell phone?"

"Had one," Joshua admitted forlornly, "but it fell into the loo when I took a leak in the restroom of a bar at the last town. It doesn't work anymore."

To Joshua's surprise, the man laughed. But it was a nasty, unsympathetic sound. "Ain't your day, mate, is it?" he jeered.

"That it ain't," Joshua agreed nervously. He projected just the right amount of uncertainty as he shifted from foot to foot and nodded toward the interior of the house. "So, can I use that phone?"

"Sorry," the man replied, his voice indicating that he was anything but. "Never got around to hooking up a service." And then he paused, as if debating. Joshua guessed that he was weighing whether it was less trouble to shoot him or get him to leave on his own. And then the man surprised him by looking over his shoulder into the house. "Hey, Ken," the man shouted. "C'mere."

A moment later, "Ken," a lanky man whose clothes were meant for someone a size or two larger in build, shuffled to the front door. It was obvious by his manner that he didn't like being summoned. It was also obvious that he didn't have the courage not to come when called.

He looked sullenly at the intruder, then at the man who had called him. "Yeah?"

"Why don't you play the Good Samaritan and see if you can help this bloke with his car." The man sounded almost genial. But his voice was flat and unreadable as he added, "Says it's dead. Go check it out."

The man probably asks his mother for an ID, Joshua thought.

Ken's sullen expression deepened. "Why the hell should I?"

"Because I said so," the man bit off. Then he

looked at the man on his right. "Ken here can fix anything, can't you, Ken?"

Ken's answer was given under his breath and addressed to his shoes as he shuffled onto the front porch. He turned up the collar of his dark shirt against the rain, as if that would make a difference. "Where is it?" he wanted to know.

Joshua pointed north. "About a mile or so down the road."

Ken cursed roundly, then told the man in the doorway, "I'm taking the van."

In response, the first man pulled a set of keys out of his pants pocket.

"Take my car instead," he instructed in a firm monotone that allowed for no argument.

Ken grudgingly accepted the keys and trudged off to the tan car parked over to the extreme right side of the front yard.

Joshua nodded his thanks at the man in the doorway and quickly followed behind Ken. In a move that would have made a magician proud, he'd already shifted his weapon to the side to avoid having it detected as he walked away.

Fifteen minutes later, Joshua was back at the house. This time, however, he didn't knock on the front door. He approached the farmhouse from the rear. He'd left the sullen Ken bound, gagged and unconscious in the front seat of the now disabled tan vehicle. Cars didn't go very far without their distributor caps.

One down and he wasn't certain how many more to go, but at least there was one less gun to face. He had Ken's tucked beside his own. The metal chafed his skin.

Above him, a lightning bolt flashed. Thunder exploded loudly not more than thirty seconds later.

Close, he thought.

The world had gone crazy. There was no other explanation for the kind of weather they were having this summer.

The storm had descended and it was interfering royally with his cell phone's reception. He glanced at the cell's screen. There was no signal coming in at all. Joshua frowned. His cell phone was temporarily useless and that left him dependent solely on his own ingenuity.

He'd been in worse situations.

His boots sinking into dirt now rendered to mud, Joshua gingerly tried the window. Locked, it didn't budge. Quickly stripping off his shirt, he wrapped it around his arm, then swung it, breaking the glass with his elbow just as another crack of thunder resounded.

Despite the cover of thunder, the woman in the chair abruptly turned her head in his direction.

Joshua lost no time reaching in and unlocking the window. Raising the sash, he slipped into the dust mote laden room.

Her eyes were green, he noted. And huge as they watched and absorbed his every move.

Huge, but not frightened.

Good. The last thing he wanted was a hysterical woman he couldn't reason with on his hands. Even if she was gorgeous.

Oh, God, now what? Pru thought, her breath backing up into her lungs. They're coming out of the woodwork, or at least through the windows.

Her adrenaline kicked into overtime at this latest threat. She'd been working on her ropes now for God only knew how long, ever since that cretin in the baggy clothes had come in with a tray of what looked like recycled table scraps. He'd had the audacity to offer to feed her with the promise of a "special dessert if you behave yourself."

The laugh that followed had made her skin crawl.

As he came toward her, she'd managed to twist and bump into him, knocking the tray out of his hands. It, the plate of food and the dirty glass of water had crashed to the floor. The latter had shattered.

Just as she'd hoped.

Cursing her, her kidnapper had picked up the pieces. All but the one shard she'd covered with her sneaker and drew beneath her chair, leaving her foot over it.

It had taken time and patience, patience when she wanted nothing more than to flee, but she'd counted off thirty minutes. Thirty minutes before she executed the second part of her plan. Rocking back and forth, she'd finally succeeded in tipping over her chair. When she crashed to the floor, she'd felt the impact reverberating in her teeth, not to mention through her shoulders.

The crash had brought her kidnappers running, then cursing, then finally laughing at her. She assumed that they thought she was attempting to break the chair and then escape. They'd called her stupid and told her not to try anything like that again, then left. She hardly heard them, aware only of the shard of glass she'd secured and now held locked in her closed fist.

The moment the door was closed, she went to work.

It was slow, tedious and painful. Pru worked the shard like a tiny, jagged glass saw, drawing it back and forth across the thick hemp that held her prisoner, feeling a sticky trickle of blood at her wrist. She'd just managed to cut through the ropes when this miscreant had come through the window.

A new face. Another one of the kidnappers?

She wasn't sure how many there were and only knew two by actual sight. His coming through the window made no sense, unless he didn't want the others to know what he was doing.

Every muscle in her body tensed.

She pretended to still be bound as the stranger came toward her. The element of surprise was all she had.

He put his finger to his lips, as if the dolt thought she could scream beneath the duct tape. If she could have screamed, she would have done so a long time ago. Loud and long.

He crouched down beside her. He was going to rape her, she thought, banking down the surge of panic and turning it into fury. He damn well might try, but he was going to lose a few vital organs in the process.

"This is going to hurt," he warned her, taking the edge of the duct tape covering her mouth in his fingers. He yanked it quickly and a line of fiery pain zigzagged along her lips.

The next second, she propelled herself forward, lunging at him. He wound up on the floor, flat on his back, with her on top of him, pinning him down.

"This'll hurt more," she declared fiercely, her face inches from his.

Her heart pounding wildly, Prudence began to scramble to her feet, intent on grabbing the weapon she'd seen go flying from his waistband. But he caught her wrists with his hands and held her to him. The length of his rock-hard body directly beneath hers registered on the outer perimeter of her consciousness. As did the heat from his bare chest.

Stockholm syndrome, Stockholm syndrome, she warned herself. He was a lowlife, nothing else.

A lowlife with a temper.

"Are you out of your mind?" he hissed angrily.

She squirmed and wriggled against him, trying to get free, alarmed at the sensations that were swiftly and dramatically telegraphing themselves through her body. Alarmed, too, at the rather sensual curve of his mouth as he looked up at her.

Prudence gathered her indignation to her like an invisible, invincible cloak. She was *not* about to succumb to this. They were *not* going to keep her docile and inline with this cheap ploy. She didn't care how hard his chest, or other parts of him for that matter, were.

"If you think that I'm just going to lie here and let you attack me, you less than worthless sack of horse manure, then—"

"Attack you?" he echoed incredulously, his hands still very tightly wrapped around her wrists where they would remain until he was confident that she wasn't going to take a swing at him. "I'm here to rescue you."

For a moment, still sprawled out on top of him, Pru wavered. Rescue her? She was being rescued? Her father had actually managed to find where she was being held? The man deserved more credit than she'd been giving him lately.

And then suspicion crept in between the lines.

"Where are the others?" she wanted to know.

"There are no others," he told her.

Her eyes widened. "You're it?"

"Yup. Lucky me," the man commented dryly. "Now, not that I wouldn't find this position interesting at any other time—" he opened his hands, releasing her wrists "—but I think that we'd better get the hell out of here before one of those Neanderthals comes to investigate the noise."

Pru scrambled to her feet, managing to have more than just marginal contact with all parts of him. "Just who the hell are you?" she demanded hotly, her cheeks burning.

A smile twisted the man's lips as he motioned her over to the same window he'd just used to get in. "At the moment," he told her, "your savior."

Chapter 4

If Pru was going to respond to the information this bare-chested, unmasked avenger had just flippantly tossed at her, the opportunity was snatched from her.

She heard a noise behind her but before she could turn around to see what was happening, the man with the washboard abs was grabbing her by the wrist again and yanking her so that she was suddenly behind him. The snub-nosed weapon was in his hand so quickly, she didn't even see where it had come from. All she knew was that it was there, being aimed at the man who had just walked into the bedroom.

The next moment, the man had fallen to his

knees, a single hole very neatly placed in the center of his forehead.

Shock and wonder vibrated all through her. "You killed him," she cried.

"That's the idea." And then the stranger was pushing her toward the open window. "Let's go!" he ordered in a voice that would have made a marine drill sergeant proud.

Ever since she could remember, Pru had always hated being ordered around. Hated being rendered to the state of an inanimate object, thought unable to think for herself.

But there was no arguing with the wisdom behind the soggy Adonis's command.

Later she'd take him to task for his irreverent manhandling of her. Right now, all she wanted to do was put an infinite amount of distance between herself and the men she knew in her heart were going to kill her whenever they decided that she'd ceased to be useful to them.

Pru was drenched half a second after she'd exited through the window.

The ground was soft and muddy, the sky completely covered with black, ominous clouds that were relentlessly draining themselves over the land. She was about to ask which way to run, assuming that this man had an escape plan mapped out, when he grabbed her wrist for a third time and, in a dead run, began to drag her in his wake. Prudence had no doubt that if she fell, this man would just drag her behind him in the mud like some broken, dysfunctional pull toy.

She glared at the back of his soaked, dark head. If he was her rescuer, or her savior as he claimed, he certainly had never been to knight-in-shining-armor school.

Behind them, the rest of her kidnappers must have rushed into the back room, drawn by the sound of the single gunshot. Making an immediate assessment, they'd run to the window and began firing.

Bullets were flying at them like lethal mosquitoes on steroids.

"You should have used a silencer!" Prudence shouted at the back of her rescuer's head, raising her voice to be heard above the gunfire, the thunder and whatever else nature in its perverse capriciousness had decided to throw at them.

"I'll have to remember that for next time," he shouted back.

They reached what must be his vehicle and Pru's "savior" threw open the passenger door and shoved her in, then slid across the hood to get to the driver's side. He seemed to stumble and clutched his leg, but then jumped in the car.

"What are you, a *Dukes of Hazard* wannabe?" she asked incredulously. "Never mind," Pru retorted when her remark earned her a puzzled scowl, adding urgently, "Get this thing started."

"That's what I'm doing," he told her as he turned

the key in the ignition. After one false cough, the car came to life.

"Hurry, get us out of here," Pru cried, craning her neck to look back toward the farmhouse.

One of the men was tumbling out the window, head first. The other was already out and racing across the field toward the van. Prudence sucked in her breath as she saw the man whom she took to be the ringleader get into the van. He'd been the one who was driving yesterday morning when they'd dragged her off the path.

Her stomach twisted into a knot even though she refused to give in to panic. "Oh, God, they're coming after us."

"What did you expect?" her rescuer asked. Tires squealed as he hit the road.

Only then did she remember to buckle up. She pushed the metal tongue into its slot. "A S.W.A.T. team, not a half-naked man."

"Sorry," he told her. "The realm is fresh out of S.W.A.T. teams at the moment." Stepping on the gas, he slanted a quick glance in her direction. "What part do you object to? That I'm half-naked or half-dressed?"

Oh, God, heaven spare her. Another man with an ego. "I object to the fact that my father sent a Neanderthal to rescue me."

His mouth curved in a smile that remained exclusively on his lips and nowhere else. "Sorry, James Bond was busy dallying with a woman who knew that you catch more flies with honey than you do with vinegar."

Restrained by the seat belt, she still twisted around in her seat, looking out the back window and holding her breath as she tried to focus through the sheets of falling rain.

"Is that the way you think of yourself? As being a honey-deprived fly?" But before he could make any sort of a cryptic retort in response, Prudence realized something. The van wasn't moving. Wide-eyed, she looked from the rear window to the driver on her right. "They're not coming after us. Why aren't they coming after us?"

Instead of answering, the dripping driver with the hard body leaned over into her space. She was about to push him back when, one hand still on the wheel, he flipped open the glove compartment. Two round, plastic-looking things tumbled out onto her wet lap. She had no idea what they were.

"I think these might have something to do with it." He caught the confused expression on her face as he straightened again. "They're distributor caps."

Pru came to the only conclusion she could. "So the van's disabled?"

"Unless one of them's got a spare distributor cap in their pocket."

Spinning the steering wheel around, the man executed a 270-degree turn and sped off in a new direction. Plumes of water flew up on either side of the vehicle while sheets of rain continued to come down.

The road, when they finally reached it, was slippery, threatening to wrench control of the car away at the first unguarded moment.

He put the windshield wipers on high and they urgently began to duel with the rain. "You picked a hell of a day to be kidnapped."

That she was rescued had not yet actually sunk in. The sensation was further impeded by the fact that she wasn't completely sold that they were out of danger, no matter what the bare-chested man said about the distribution hats, or distributor caps, or whatever those things he'd taken off with were.

Prudence shoved both items back into the glove compartment, fighting with the door to get it closed. She was too full of adrenaline, too full of fury, to relax. And his smart mouth wasn't helping the situation any.

"Next time I'll have the kidnappers check the weather report before they abduct me," she snapped, shifting in the wet seat.

He spared her a quick look, then shook his head. She caught the latter and it only served to further fuel her anger. "You really do have a sunny personality, don't you?"

The mean-spirited nickname she'd been awarded immediately crossed her mind. Her eyes narrowed as she looked at his damn-near-perfect profile. Probably had women falling all over him. "What's that supposed to mean?"

"That sometimes the tabloids get it right."

She stiffened, pressing her lips together as she pushed a fallen wet strand out of her eyes. God, but she was tired of having to defend herself, of having her every move scrutinized and found lacking by someone. And when the truth didn't live up to expectations, there were always lies to use.

Her voice was monotone and weary as she said, "I had you pegged as someone who reads trash."

"And just when did you make this character assessment, Prudence? When I crashed into the room to rescue you or when I used my body as a human shield as they were shooting at you?"

For a second, there was nothing but the sound of the rain, beating against the windshield and the noise of the tires as they struggled against the ever-softening ground. Prudence flushed. He was right. She was being incredibly waspish. Living up to, she realized, all the nasty stories that were written about her. Stories that were taken out of context because the public demanded its daily dose of gossip, whether or not it was true.

She took a deep breath, then said, almost in a whisper, "Sorry."

"What was that?" He took one hand off the steering wheel and cupped it to the ear closest to her. "I didn't quite hear you. Sounded like you said you were sorry."

She didn't know whether to laugh at him or hit him. She wanted to do both. Instead, she settled for warning him. "Don't push it."

"Wouldn't dream of it," he quipped.

Joshua glanced in the rearview mirror. In the

distance, on the road, he could just barely make out the beams of two headlights foreshadowing an advancing vehicle.

Had there been a third car somewhere? A car he hadn't seen?

There'd been no time to go scouting into the barn or the garage. Now he wished he had.

Stepping all the way down on the accelerator, he drove as if it were a foregone conclusion that they were being followed by her abductors.

"Damn."

Prudence jerked like a piece of toast popping out of its toaster. Twisting around in her seat, she looked behind at the road.

"Is that them?" she wanted to know. "Are they following us?"

Ordinarily, he'd say something to comfort the kidnap victim. But Pru didn't strike him as someone who would appreciate being lied to or hearing half truths. So he shrugged and gave it to her straight. "I don't know. Maybe."

"I thought you said you disabled the cars." Her tone was nothing short of accusing.

Maybe he should have lied to her. "The ones I could see."

She looked panicked. "Were there more?"

At this point he had no way of knowing with any certainty. "There could have been."

"*Could* have been?" she repeated incredulously. "Isn't it your job to know?"

He'd had just about enough of her carping. It was hard enough maneuvering in this weather on these roads without having to deal with her as well.

"Look, this wasn't exactly D-day at Normandy. I didn't have days to plan out your rescue. Approximately thirty-six hours ago, I was sleeping in my own bed, blissfully unaware of you as anything other than an occasional headline to my right as I deposited my groceries onto the conveyor belt at my local supermarket."

His repeated references to the tabloids seemed to make her bristle. "And now here we are, cozier than two peas in a pod."

"Or at least wetter than the aforementioned peas." He dragged his hand through his hair, sending a small spray of water flying in her direction.

She put up a hand. "Hey," she protested.

He raised a shoulder in a careless shrug, then let it drop. "Sorry, didn't think you'd notice a little more water."

"Can't you make this thing go faster?" she asked impatiently.

"Not without a pilot's license. Besides, if I go any faster," he said from between gritted teeth, "I could lose control of the car."

She had one better for him. "If you don't go any faster, you might lose control over *us.*"

"I wasn't aware that anyone actually had control over you." The retort came without thought. And from the look on her face when he glanced toward her, it had struck a nerve. "Sorry, didn't mean to insult you."

"Why stop now?"

"Look, I'm the guy who just risked his neck to rescue you." He felt the vehicle begin to fishtail and he gripped the wheel, driving into the curve. A minute later, he straightened the wheel. "Shouldn't you be nicer to me than this?"

He had a feeling she hated being wrong. Was she woman enough to admit it?

"You're right. I should. Kidnappings make me nervous."

"Yeah, me, too." Since she'd mellowed for a moment, so could he. "This your first?" He was making conversation. There was very little about Prudence Hill that he didn't know. It had all been succinctly captured for him between the pages of the dossier he'd been given. He'd managed to read all of it before they'd landed, having trained himself in speed reading just before joining the Lazlo Group.

She began to answer in the negative. He knew that there had been one previous incident, when she was a little girl and not yet the prime minister's daughter. The plot had been quickly foiled.

He expected her to explain, but Pru turned her face toward the window on her side. "Yes."

Since she didn't bring it up, neither did he. "Well, it's not mine. As far as kidnappings go, this is coming along quite nicely for our side."

"'Our' side? Last time I looked, I was the one who'd been kidnapped, not you."

"For the time being," he informed her, ignoring her tone, "we're a team. Only difference between us being that, should those be your former kidnappers behind us and they manage to catch up, you'll be taken prisoner again. I'll be killed," he added with no emotion.

She actually looked at him with concern. "I hadn't thought of that."

He nodded, keeping his eyes on the darkened road. "Didn't think so."

A wall rose up between them like a tower of cotton swabs suddenly filled with water. "Are you saying that I'm insensitive?"

Oh no, he wasn't about to get sucked into this verbal waltz. "I'm saying that most kidnap victims don't think beyond their own immediate situation."

"I am not a victim."

He hadn't said it to take a dig at her. It was just the way things were. "Didn't look to me as if you had the upper hand back there."

Pru drew back her shoulders. "For your information, I had just cut through my ropes."

He laughed shortly, then found himself narrowly avoiding battling a tree for the same physical space. Turning at the last minute, he let out a sigh of relief. That had been close. "With what, your X-ray vision?"

"With a piece of glass that I got by making one

of those oafs drop a tray when he came into the room to feed me," she informed him tersely.

He looked at her for a split second before returning his attention to the road. The headlights, he noted, were still behind them. No closer, no farther.

"Go on," he encouraged. "I'm curious how it got from the floor to your hand."

"I tilted the chair until it fell and then picked the shard up."

He nodded, taking it all in. "And what was the guy with the tray doing all this time?"

"He'd already left." She sounded close to being on the verge of eruption. "What kind of an idiot do you take me for?"

He had an answer for that. "One who refuses a bodyguard when her father has the key deciding vote on a hotly contested bill that's currently on the floor in Parliament."

She blew out a breath. "So you've been briefed."

His mouth curved. "In a manner of speaking."

"Just who the hell are you? And don't give me that tripe about being my savior. Saviors wear more clothes," she informed him tersely before he could say anything.

His smile deepened. "My name's Joshua Lazlo."

"Lazlo," she repeated. "That's—"

"Hungarian," he supplied.

"You're Hungarian?" She looked at him, marginal confusion echoing in her gaze.

"I'm a British citizen, born and bred," he told her.

"Of British parents," he added lest there was any question of his allegiance.

"Why don't I find that comforting?"

"You're going to have to figure that out for yourself."

She sighed again and lowered her eyes. Suddenly they widened. "You're bleeding."

He glanced down to where she was looking. And shrugged. That would explain the sharp pain in his thigh and why it continued to feel as if it were on fire, he thought.

"Looks that way."

"Were you shot?" she asked incredulously.

He kept his voice devoid of emotion, as if they were talking about scones. "That would be my guess."

She lost her patience. "My God, what are you, the British Clint Eastwood? Do you have a handkerchief?" she demanded. "What am I saying, you don't even have a shirt."

She looked around the interior of the vehicle, opening the glove compartment and rummaging through it. Then, muttering under her breath, she raised the hem of her T-shirt and bit into it where the seams came together, tugging on either side as she did so.

He watched her out of the corner of his eye, amused. "There's a simpler way, you know." She stopped and looked at him. "Just raise it over your head and toss it off. You don't have to rip it off with your teeth."

Pru glared at him, saying nothing. The next second, the material began to tear. To his astonishment, she forced it along horizontally, swiftly reducing her T-shirt to a belly shirt.

"There," she declared in triumph. She held the strip between her hands. "All right, raise your leg," she ordered.

He kept his attention on the road, realizing she meant to use her shirt as a bandage. "Your bedside manner leaves something to be desired."

"Obviously everything is a big joke to you. Well, you aren't about to bleed to death on my account. Do as you're told."

"Yes, ma'am," he replied meekly, raising his thigh as far as he could off the seat while still keeping his foot on the pedal.

Pru snorted at the polite term. "That'll get you a kick where you really don't want one," she warned him as she secured the bandage around his thigh.

She pulled too tight and he jerked before he could stop himself. The car went out of control, its wheels all but flying off the road.

The front of the vehicle took a nosedive down the embankment and kept on going despite Joshua's best efforts to stop it.

Chapter 5

The car's downward slide was fast and furious. Hanging on to the steering wheel, Joshua did what he could to guide the vehicle down the steep incline, praying that it wouldn't flip over. He was vaguely aware that his heart was pounding in his ears.

And then the vehicle came to a sudden, abrupt halt near the bottom of the incline, close to a heavily wooded area. Trying to take in everything and quickly assess the situation, Joshua was vaguely surprised that the person next to him hadn't screamed.

He had a bad feeling about that.

Pain shot through his skull, originating where his forehead had made jolting contact with the air bag.

The fact that he felt pain was a good thing. It meant he wasn't dead.

He had amnesia for exactly three seconds. And then everything came crowding back into his brain.

The prime minister's daughter.

Instantly, Joshua was working his seat belt loose, trying to turn in her direction. From what he could make out, it looked as if the air bag was in the process of swallowing her.

"Are you all right?" he demanded. When she didn't answer, Joshua felt the last bit of his adrenaline shooting through his veins. With effort, he pushed aside his air bag and elbowed his way beneath hers. "Prudence. Prudence," he repeated more urgently, taking her hand and massaging her arm, trying to get her circulation going. She was unconscious. It was impossible to see if she was breathing, there wasn't enough light. "C'mon, open your eyes. Open your eyes for me, Prudence."

And then he detected a small flutter. Her lids raised ever so slightly.

"Why?" she asked thickly. "So you can drive off another cliff?"

He sighed, relieved. She was alive. And grumpy as ever. Joshua dropped her hand.

"Yeah, you're all right," he muttered. "And it was an incline, not a cliff."

Pru tried to take a deep breath. The air bag was in her way. "My mistake. Hard to tell the difference at a hundred miles an hour in a monsoon."

The accusatory note in her voice irritated Joshua beyond words. "You're the one who wanted me to go faster."

He didn't bother reminding her that had she not been attempting to bandage his thigh, they might not have gone off the side of the road and down the incline in the first place. There was no point in taking her to task for her one act of compassion. It might disincline her from ever performing another one.

"Right," Pru muttered.

She put her hand to her aching forehead, trying to focus. The rain was beginning to let up. She didn't know if that was a good thing or not, considering that they still might have pursuers and the poor visibility could only act in their favor.

If it didn't get them lost first.

As she tried to move, Pru felt the seat belt cutting into her, refusing to give. Feeling around to the side, she found the release button. Except that it didn't. No matter how hard she pressed the button, the belt stayed where it was.

"Is this hell?" she wanted to know, addressing the question to Joshua.

"Pretty much," he acknowledged. If this were heaven, he would have been trapped in a car with one of the scores of young women who made his life so pleasurable, not Pru the Shrew. "Get your seat belt off and let's see if we can get out of here."

"What do you think I'm trying to do?" she snapped. She hit the release button one more time, then yanked at the seat belt. Neither would give. "It won't open." The words were no sooner out of her mouth than she saw Joshua unbuckling his belt and pulling it out of the loops of his slacks. Something skittered through her stomach. She banked it down and demanded, "What do you think you're doing?"

"Easy, Pru," Joshua said in a patronizing tone that made her want to punch him out if she could only reach him. "I'm not about to have my way with you. I'm getting this."

"This" was a knife attached to the inside of his belt buckle and carefully folded against the leather. Before she could say anything to the effect that most men, if they carried a knife at all, had it as part of a Swiss Army set that resided in their pockets, he'd taken his knife by the hilt and imbedded the blade in her air bag. The bag collapsed instantly, giving him better access to her.

One swift pass and she and the seat belt parted company.

"You *are* useful," she commented, hoping that the flippant remark covered just how relieved she was to be set free.

"So they tell me." Slipping the belt back on, Joshua tried his door. Although the handle moved, the door didn't. Smashed into the body of the vehicle along the lower edge, it refused to budge. He put his shoulder to it, but got the same results. Frustrated, he looked at the passenger door. "Let's see if yours works." He gave Pru no chance to pull back. Leaning the length of his body over her side of the vehicle, he grabbed the door handle.

"I can open my door," she informed him, using her shoulder to push him back. She took hold of the handle and pushed it down. Or tried to. It wouldn't give.

Joshua watched her go through the motions three times before asking, "What's the matter?"

"I can't open my door." Pru ground out the words grudgingly. "It's stuck."

He tried it himself and came to the same exasperating conclusion. The windows were both automated. Turning the key in the ignition did not bring the vehicle back to life. The windows remained where they were. Sealed.

A sense of claustrophobia, not to mention alarm, was setting in. Pru could feel her breath growing short. She turned to look at the man next to her. "Think of something," she ordered.

Joshua was quickly beginning to believe that someone up there was trying to make him pay for his errant ways. "Well, since you put it so nicely— what the hell do you think I'm doing?"

She glared at him. If she concentrated on being angry, she reasoned, she wouldn't have time to be afraid. "Failing."

Joshua didn't trust himself to answer her. An idea had come to him. Still seething, he leaned back in the driver's side, then slid down until his shoulders were almost on the seat and his feet were raised up above the top of the steering wheel.

Pru stared at him incredulously. He looked as if he was doing some kind of outlandish exercise. "What—?"

Joshua didn't wait for her to frame a question. Given her track record, it would probably be insulting and he was in no mood to hear it.

"Trying to get us out of here before I strangle my assignment," he informed her tersely.

With that, he kicked at the windshield with both feet as hard as he could. Nothing happened. He did it again. And again. And again. The impact reverberated in his thigh, sending shafts of pain shooting through his leg. He did what he could to block it. He couldn't let the pain stop him. As far as he could see, this was their only way out.

From the corner of his eye, he saw Pru sliding down in her seat and raising her legs up, emulating him. "What are *you* doing?" he demanded.

"Two sets of feet are better than one," she retorted, pounding both feet against the windshield.

He grinned. "There's hope for you yet, Prudence."

Pru hated being called by her full given name. She took her ire out on the windshield.

He'd almost lost count the number of times they kicked the windshield when the surface suddenly dissolved into a thousand tiny spiderlike veins, fanning out to cover the entire area.

Enthused, he shouted, "Again!"

"No kidding, Sherlock," Pru retorted audibly under her breath.

Two more times did it.

Glass went flying out and rain, now just a fine mist, immediately came in.

"We're free!" Pru cried, elated.

She almost looked human then, Joshua thought. Pulling his boot off, he quickly moved it along the perimeter of the windshield, getting rid of as much of the glass as possible.

He went through first, wincing as glass he'd missed scraped along his bare skin and snagged his pants. But that was the point of going first, to keep the cuts *she* sustained to a minimum.

Twisting around on the hood to face her, Joshua extended his hand to the prime minister's daughter and his newest cross to bear.

"Let's go," he instructed.

He didn't have to say it twice. She was out and onto the hood in a blink of an eye. If any of the glass cut into her, she didn't indicate it. Grabbing her by the waist, Joshua helped her down. She didn't weigh all that much, he thought. Was she one of those weight-conscious women who threw up all their meals? No, on second thought, he had a feeling she didn't care what other people thought of her.

"Let's go," he said again the second her feet touched the ground. The next moment, they were sliding down the short path to the flat ground, away from the demolished vehicle. The actual road was high above them, but right now it was safer down here.

"Which way?" Pru wanted to know.

Joshua was surprised that she didn't insist on taking the lead. Maybe the woman did have the sense she was born with.

"That way." He pointed south and explained, "I saw a cottage back there when I drove past earlier." And it had looked exactly like that, a cottage out of a quaint fairy tale.

Pru turned south. "Cottage it is."

He nodded, noting that, for the first time since he'd taken her duct tape off, the prime minister's daughter wasn't giving him an argument.

"What do you mean you lost them?" Cassandra DuMont demanded sharply, her well-manicured fingernails all but digging into the surface of the highly polished mahogany desk she was leaning over. She glared at the wide flat panel mounted on the opposite wall. Glared at the man she saw in it, shifting uncomfortably as he called in the new development.

The man calling her headed the team that had been sent to abduct the British prime minister's daughter. Though this was the sort of assignment the organization she now helmed undertook, this particular time it was also to set another spoke of her plan into motion. The first had already been satisfactorily carried out, but the same could not be said for this.

For her to have what she wanted, what had been her heart's prime focus for so many years now, it all had to work, not just parts.

The man on the screen hesitated. If he were actually in the room with her, he would have towered over the woman from whom he took orders. That did not alter the fact that he feared her.

They all did.

They knew she could kill in cold blood without blinking an eye. Brilliant, she was deemed completely unpredictable. No one could say with any certainty what she would do next. She could embrace someone or stab him, it was all the same to her. She made sure her employees understood that. It was best to remain on the good side of someone like her as much as possible.

"It's just temporary," he promised.

Cassandra raised her chin and narrowed her green eyes into small, deadly slits. "Oh, like your life."

She watched as the single sentence cut him to the quick like a sharp knife. Good. Her meaning was crystal clear. If Prudence Hill was not found and found quickly, his life would be forfeited.

Cassandra did not trouble herself with empty threats. There were no "do-overs" in her book. She'd become more deadly than her father, from whom she wrested control of his organization on his death bed. Payback for the fact that nothing she ever did seemed good enough to him. She'd lived in the shadow of the brother who had died years ago, the brother whose death her father never got over, saying more than once that it should have been her who died, not Apollo.

Cassandra did nothing to dispel the rumor that she had hastened the old man's steady decline with a salad dressing liberally sprinkled with finely crushed oleanders. If she could do that to her own flesh and blood, then no one was safe.

The fact that she had shed tears at his funeral only compounded that feeling.

"We'll get her back," the man on the screen promised with feeling.

She kept her eyes cold, flat, as she said, "See that you do."

Nerves were evident in his voice as he asked, "Do you want a report?"

She waved a dismissive hand, sweeping away the question. "I'm not interested in hearing about your failures, Conrad. Only your successes." She drew her finely shaped eyebrows into one commanding line. "The next time you call, you'd better be ready to tell me that you have her."

With that, she terminated the teleconference, cursing less than softly under her breath. Her one show of temper was to send a stack of papers on her desk flying, courtesy of the back of her hand.

"Incompetent imbeciles. I'm surrounded with incompetent imbeciles."

"You should have sent me to get the PM's brat. She wouldn't have gotten away from me."

Cassandra looked up to see Troy, the blond boy she had presented to her father as her adopted son nineteen years ago, walking into her office. Each time she saw him, she was struck by how handsome he had become. How tall, how self-possessed. And how eager to show everyone what he was made of.

Too eager, she thought. *And when you are too eager, you make mistakes.*

Her son was not to make mistakes. Not because she was demanding, but because she could brook no one saying anything against Troy. He was her pride and joy, the single thing that made everything she had been through worthwhile.

Troy's raw eagerness both amused her and made her proud. When the time came, she would use that eagerness to deliver the death blow. It would be incredibly satisfying and supremely poetic.

But for now, she intended to keep Troy reined in. "All in good time, my dear, all in good time." She beckoned him to her. When he came, she slipped her arm around his shoulder, completing the circle that was just the two of them. "You need seasoning."

Troy frowned petulantly. She knew he was tired of the excuses, tired of being treated like a child when he was a man. He wanted to prove himself.

"The way to get seasoning is in the field." Turning, he shrugged her off and faced her. "How am I supposed to live up to my heritage if you insist on protecting me?" It was an accusation.

The smile on Cassandra's lips had frozen the blood in more than one man's veins. She didn't like being challenged, wouldn't stand for it. But this was Troy, the only male she had taken to her heart since the last one had betrayed her twenty years ago. And so she smiled tolerantly at her eager foot soldier.

"You sit and you learn, Troy, like a good student. You sit and you learn," she repeated. "And when the time is right, you will take your place in the organization. No one will take it from you."

He raised his chin, an exact copy of the way she raised hers. Defiant. "And how will we know when the time is right?"

She looked at him with eyes that Corbett Lazlo had once found both mesmerizing and penetrating. There was not a single thread of doubt in her voice as she told him, "*I* will know. And I will tell you."

"Anything yet?"

So engrossed in trying to untangle what was so hopelessly tangled before her, Lucia Cordez, the Lazlo Group's computer expert par excellence, hadn't heard her boss enter the room.

The man moved like smoke, she thought. It was a hold over from his early days in MI-6, where he had gotten his initial training. It wasn't until Lazlo spoke that she even knew he was there.

As he asked the question, Lazlo absently placed his hand on her shoulder, looking over her to his computer screen.

Lucia tried not to react to the soft pressure, the slight, fleeting contact that registered so intently, causing the hiccup in her stomach. She doubted that Lazlo was even aware that he had placed his hand there as he peered at the screen. Actual physical contact was not his way.

For the most part, her employer was removed. It was what made him Lazlo, a mystery that none of them were ever going to solve. Unless he wanted them to. Which she sincerely doubted.

Taking a discreet breath to still the momentary flutter, Lucia focused on the blue screen. It'd had her full, undivided attention since Lazlo had called her in this morning and shown her the single ominous line printed in the middle of it.

Now the screen was filled with all kinds of coding, none of which, unfortunately, was getting her any closer to finding where the message had originally come from or who had sent it. The only thing that was crystal clear was that whoever had sent it had covered his or her tracks with the meticulous care of a government agent whose very life depended upon his ability to preserve his nonentity and remain invisible.

Lucia rotated her neck from side to side, warding off the encroaching stiffness. For all she knew, the threat could have come from someone associated with one of the world agencies they dealt with. A disgruntled agent who had been uncovered to his superiors due to the investigative efforts of one of the operatives with the Lazlo Group.

Or it could have been sent by someone with a personal vendetta against one of them, if not Lazlo himself. The agents who worked for Lazlo were not careful when it came to treading on toes if those toes were in the way of bringing a mission to a successful conclusion. And they always, always accomplished their mission. Sometimes quickly, sometimes not so quickly, but the outcome, once the Lazlo Group was brought into it, was never in doubt. That was why they were hired and why their unorthodox methods were accepted.

But success, achieved their way, did tend to yield a hefty crop of enemies.

Lucia leaned back against her seat, staring at the screen, willing it to all come together.

"Not yet," she confessed, answering his ambiguous question.

She hated the taste of the negative words as she uttered them. Lucia stifled the urge to drag her hand through her long, dark curly hair. That was a tell, a sign of nervousness, and Lazlo preferred his people steady. It was just that she was accustomed to getting whatever was asked of her done in a matter of a few hours. This was going to be different.

"Whoever this is," she tapped the screen, "is damn good."

"Apparently," Lazlo agreed, his voice emotionless. "But you're better."

She smiled. A compliment. The rarest of things when it came to Lazlo. But then, he and she had been together for quite some time. He had been, quite literally, her Svengali. Blessed with both brains and beauty, she had used the former and hidden the latter. Until Lazlo had found her and recruited her near-genius with the computer for his newly formed group. Taking her in hand, he'd taught her how to make the most of all her assets, to be proud of her looks and bring attention to them.

Men, sadly, did not expect a beautiful woman to be intelligent—and that was her ace in the hole. She'd thought at the time, as she trained and learned all the skills that went into being a successful agent destined to live a long life, that he was training her to be a field operative. But despite all her training and despite the fact that she knew several languages fluently and had exotic looks, thanks to a Latin father and a mother who was half Caucasian, half African-American, Lazlo insisted that her time be spent in the offices at the computer. There was the occasional outing, but again, as a computer expert, not as a spy.

There was a time when she'd bristled against that. Now she had come to terms with it. Lazlo used his people to their best advantage. And he always knew best. Which was why praise was so heady and so dear. Because it was so sparse.

She looked at his reflection in her screen. "You make it hard to fail, Lazlo."

"Then don't."

She closed her eyes briefly. When she turned around to reply, he was gone.

Like smoke, she thought again, then turned back to the monitor.

Chapter 6

The minute Joshua tried to actually run, he realized that there was going to be a problem. The leg with the bullet wound rebelled against supporting his weight. Instead of being able to hurry alongside Prudence, he found his leg buckling beneath him. Going down, he cursed roundly.

Already several feet ahead of him, Pru swung around and saw Joshua on the ground, one leg under the other. The first thing she thought was that they'd been discovered and someone was firing at them. But she hadn't heard any gunshots, only the rumble of the now distant thunder.

Doubling back, Pru quickly reached his side. "What's the matter?"

Joshua tried to get up, but there was nothing for him to use as leverage. "I can't run," he ground out, the answer throbbing with frustration.

It was the wound, she thought, looking at the leg she'd tried to bandage with the ripped length of cloth from the bottom of her T-shirt.

"Oh," was her only comment as her mind raced. This would be the perfect opportunity to leave him behind. Let whoever had kidnapped her deal with him. Maybe that would even buy her a little time. Besides, what did she really know about this man? For all she knew, he could have rescued her for his own reasons, reasons that had nothing whatsoever to do with getting her back to her father. Her father would have *never* sent just one man. Her father would have sent an army of men.

But what if this Joshua was what he said he was? And he *had* come to rescue her? She couldn't just leave his sorry behind here like this. He was bleeding again and there might be wild animals roaming the countryside at night, looking for prey. Wounded, Joshua would be at the top of their menu. Dinner à la carte.

So she squatted down beside him and grudgingly took his arm, drawing it around her. "Here, put your arm across my shoulders. You can use me as a crutch."

The offer offended every bone in Joshua's alpha male body. He looked around even as he rose to his feet, leaning heavily on her very slim shoulders. This just wasn't right.

"There's got to be a broken branch or something I can use for a crutch."

She was beginning to regret the offer already. "Sorry, I left my whittling tools in my other jogging shorts." Her eyebrows narrowed in a less-than-tolerant glare. "Will you stop being a macho man and let's get out of here before those cretins find us?" She started moving before she finished her sentence.

He had no choice but to move with her. He wasn't about to go anywhere on his own, at least not with any sort of speed. "All right."

"So nice of you to agree," she retorted, slipping one arm around his waist. With her other hand, she took a firmer hold of the arm that was resting across her shoulders.

She'd danced a less awkward dance in her time, Pru thought. She wanted to move fast, but that was next to impossible. Helping Lazlo cut her speed by at least half. She hoped the abductors didn't know their way around in the dark.

"Maybe you'd better leave me here," Joshua told her after several minutes.

His leg was throbbing and their progress was painfully slow. He was impeding her getaway and if the kidnappers were after her—and since this abduction was political in nature rather than just motivated by greed, there was every reason to believe that they were—then there were more people involved than just the ones back at the farmhouse. Who knew where the others were? And in his present state, he was slowing her down drastically.

"You'd like that, wouldn't you?" she bit off, doing her best not to huff and puff her words out. Being a human crutch was hard work. She could feel perspiration pasting her T-shirt to her back and her already wet hair to her forehead. If she concentrated, she could feel the drops sliding down her spine.

"What?" How could she say he'd like being left behind to the mercy of the thugs who'd already shot him? The woman wasn't making any sense. The tabloids were right about her. She *was* crazy.

Pru had a perfectly logical reason behind her accusation. She took a deep breath as the path became a little steeper. His muscles weighed a ton. Why couldn't the man have been some ninety-eight-pound weakling?

"So you can tell everyone that it's true. That that horrible nickname those awful people at the tabloids gave me is accurate."

It took him a second to remember. "You mean Pru the Shrew?"

Despite the sparse amount of moonlight, he saw her jaw tighten. He'd struck a nerve, he thought. Always good to have at least one available weapon in your arsenal.

"That's the one."

Joshua did his best not to put all of his weight on her, pivoting as much as he could on his good leg, using the momentum to propel himself along.

"Never crossed my mind," he told her. "I just didn't want to slow you down. And for your information, I never read the tabloids."

She'd caught him in a lie, she thought. "Then how would you know about the nickname?"

"The front page," he answered. "The magazines are at the checkout stands. I can't help but take in my surroundings."

"The checkout stands?" she repeated, measuring out her breaths. A misstep had her nearly twisting her ankle, but she righted herself in time. She turned to look at him and was struck by the fact that his face was much too close to hers. But there was nothing she could do about it, short of dropping him. "As in the supermarket?"

"Yeah."

"You shop in the supermarket?" she asked incredulously. He'd said something about that earlier, but she really couldn't picture the man who had come pitching headfirst into that dingy back room pushing a grocery cart up and down aisles laden with neatly boxed products. She would have bet that he didn't even know where a supermarket was located.

"Yes." He couldn't quite fathom her tone. "Why, what's wrong with that?"

"Nothing." She turned her face toward the road, feeling it was better that way. But he was still looking at her and she could feel his breath on her neck. It muddled her thoughts just a little. "I just thought you'd be the type to get your meals from restaurants—or partake a service from the flat stomach of a willing—shall we say, tart?"

His mouth curved despite the pain shooting up and down his leg and exploding in both the pit of his stomach and the center of his chest. "Well, I'll be sure to give that a try sometime."

"Glad I could give you something to look forward to." His arm was beginning to weigh a ton. If she hadn't been in such good shape, she wouldn't have been able to make it even this far. She looked around, but visibility was poor, even if it wasn't pouring any longer. She didn't see a cottage or any other kind of residence. "How much farther is this place?"

He hadn't lost his bearing, but things looked different from this vantage point than when he'd been driving. "Looked to be about five minutes as the crow flies."

That did absolutely nothing for her. "How far is it if the crow is walking and dragging a wounded secret agent man with it?"

"Longer," was all he could estimate. "And by secret agent, I take it you mean S.I.S."

She began to shrug and found that the effort was too cumbersome with his arm across her shoulders. "S.I.S., MI-6, CIA, or some such alphabet soup rendition."

Joshua shook his head. He took a breath before answering. His thigh was beginning to feel as if it really was on fire. "None of the above."

For the moment, she decided to believe him. Which narrowed down the field. "Are you a mercenary, then, hiring out to the highest bidder?"

"Hardly." Agents of the Lazlo Group did not identify themselves unless it was absolutely unavoidable. The less attention brought to the group in general, the better. For now, it was enough that her father knew they were on the job. "Let's just say that I belong to a highly skilled group of people who rescue damsels in distress out of the clutches of ill-mannered ogres."

Pru stopped for a moment to look at him. "That sounds like a bad rendition of a Grimms' fairy tale. Bullet graze your head, too?" she asked sarcastically. "Who are you with, really?"

"I'm not at liberty to say right now." He saw her frown. "But if it helps any, I am on your side."

That wasn't nearly good enough for her. "I never have anyone I don't know anything about at my side, Lazlo."

He didn't think it would be wise to point out that that was exactly where he was right now, at her side. Instead, despite the sharp twinges of pain racing up and down his extremity, he moved ahead. "In this case, I'm afraid you're going to have to put up with a little mystery until we get you back to your father."

She still wasn't convinced. "Before or after the ransom?"

Joshua caught his bad leg in some underbrush, almost tripping. He bit back a vicious curse. "You think I rescued you to get a ransom?"

Pru had almost pitched forward and it took everything to remain upright. She steadied him as best she
could, her heart racing from the exertion. "Did you?"

Maybe it was time to let her in on a few things.
"Prudence, you weren't being held for ransom to
begin with."

"Then why—?" Stunned, she didn't see the root
until it was too late. This time it was Joshua who kept
her from falling. Unlike him, she didn't hold her
tongue. The air turned blue as they stopped a second
to regroup.

Amused, Joshua asked, "Your father know you
curse like a sailor?"

She was tired, cold, hungry and wet. Not the best
of conditions for an even temper. "My father knows
very little about me," she snapped, hurt feelings
rising to the fore. "He is wrapped up in politics, his
second wife and his 'other' children, in that order."

Joshua caught the absence of Pru in that lineup.
She was feeling sorry for herself. Under the circumstances, he supposed she was entitled. But too much
of that would definitely get in their way.

"That's not true, you know. He's worried, very
worried about you."

Pru shook her head. She knew better. "He's
worried about the effect this will have on his career."
She didn't want to talk about it anymore. Something
more important needed addressing. "You said something about my not being held for ransom. Then why
were they holding me?"

He hesitated a moment, then decided she needed to know what she was up against. That she'd been a bargaining chip. "To get your father to vote down the sanctions bill he's been backing."

She laughed shortly, focusing on putting one foot in front of the other. God, she hoped they were going in the right direction. "They don't know my father very well, do they?"

She really didn't know how much she meant to the PM, did she?

"Apparently you don't, either," he told her. She looked at him. He could feel her breath along his face. She was struggling and he felt bad about it. Not to mention that his pride was taking a beating. "Because he told me he's going to have to vote the bill down unless I find you and bring you back."

She was stunned. This was her father's baby, the cornerstone of what he believed in. "My father actually said this?"

Joshua nodded, then said, "Unless the British government has learned how to effectively clone their upper officials."

"Almost makes this worth it," she murmured, then stumbled again. She took a deep breath, getting a better grip on him. When were they going to get to this so-called cottage he'd seen? "Damn, but you are heavy."

It made him feel guilty and frustrated at the same time. If anything, he should be the one carrying her, not being supported by her. "Sorry, wasn't planning on having someone drag me around."

"I'm *not* dragging," she informed him indignantly. "I'm supporting you."

He grinned, amused that she'd picked the word he'd actually thought. "And doing a fine job of it, too, Prudence."

The tone he used left Pru completely undecided as to his meaning. Was he being sincere or sarcastic? From the opinion she'd formed of him, it was most likely the latter—but his smile looked sincere.

Taking a firmer hold around his waist, trying to ignore the steady stream of perspiration snaking its way down her spine, Pru drew a long breath and prayed this journey was going to be over soon.

It wasn't soon enough.

Just as she was about to give up and just plant herself on the ground for the remainder of the night, temporarily past caring if her kidnappers found her, a small, quaint one-story building emerged from the mist. It was nestled in the middle of what appeared to be a well-tended garden.

She thought she was hallucinating, but if she was, it was a hallucination for two because the man she had her arm wrapped around suddenly came to life.

"We made it," he told her with more feeling than she herself possessed.

Pru felt close to passing out. Everything ached, and she needed food and a shower. But most of all, she needed a bed. She could have wept, seeing the small abode, but running toward it was out of the question. Aside from still supporting the secret agent, her legs felt as if they were not only lead, but belonged to someone else. She couldn't make them move any faster.

"This really does look like a cottage," she said to him as they drew closer. There was no light coming from inside, but there had to be someone there, she reasoned. There was a car parked in the front. "Something a caretaker would live in." Squinting, Pru tried to see into the distance. "Except that there is no large estate anywhere."

"That we can see," Joshua pointed out.

Since visibility was less than twenty feet ahead, she was forced to agree with him. There were no lights on, but given the hour, maybe whoever lived inside had gone to bed. If so, they could be roused.

Excited and hopeful now, Pru began to make her way up to the front door. But then she was prevented from making any further progress. Joshua had turned from a heavy weight to a lead one. He firmly resisted moving toward the door, planting his feet firmly on the ground. Obviously, the man still had some strength left, she thought, annoyed. But why pick now to demonstrate it?

When she looked at him quizzically, Joshua hissed against her ear. "What are you doing?"

Had he turned simple on her? "What does it look like I'm doing?" she snapped. "I'm going to knock on the door—"

"No," he told her firmly.

"No?" She glared at him. "*No?* Then why the hell did I just drag you heaven knows how many kilometers to get to this wretched place if we're not going to rouse the owner and get him to help us?" The bloody fool just wasn't making any sense at all.

Releasing him, she began to make her way up alone, only to have Joshua grab her firmly by the wrist and pull her back into the shadows. He hobbled as he did so, gritting his teeth, but if she thought to suddenly push him away and make a break for it, she knew it would be no easy matter. He had a grip like a steel vise.

"No," he repeated heatedly. He thought a second, casting about for a plan. He needed to call Lazlo, but his phone had no signal. Maybe he could use the phone inside the cottage. But waking whoever was staying here was not part of the plan. "Try one of the side windows."

Pru stared at him, still confused. "You mean break in?"

He nodded. "Yes."

Did all so-called spies take the hard way when there was an easier one available to them? Well, she wasn't about to blindly follow orders. She wasn't about to be ordered around at all.

"Why? Why can't we just ring the bell and wake them up?" she demanded.

Her voice was becoming audible. He pulled her to him and covered her mouth, his eyes intent on hers. "Because right now, we don't know who's involved with your abduction."

Her eyebrows drew together. Beneath his palm, she managed to query, "And you think one of the seven dwarfs is involved in it?"

It did look like a fairy-tale cottage, he thought. But that didn't change the fact that it could still belong to someone who found both their lives expendable. "Right now, everyone's a suspect until they're ruled out." Very carefully, he withdrew his hand from her mouth, watching her.

Pru shook her head. Paranoia had been part of her life for as long as she could remember. Not her own, but her father's and the bodyguard she'd had assigned to her as an adolescent. She'd never allowed it to drag her down or get in her way. Now was no exception.

"That's ridiculous."

"That's practical," Joshua countered. He held her by her arms. It was unclear to her whether it was to hold her in her place or keep himself from sinking. "Why did you think that you were brought out here instead of someplace else?"

She hadn't given the matter any thought at all. All she'd thought about was getting away. It had seemed like a simple kidnapping case to her, money in exchange for her life. Now, according to this man, there was a great deal more at stake. She'd always hated intrigue, but she couldn't exactly turn her back on it.

"I don't know," she acknowledged grudgingly.

He gave her the answer. "Because those men might have connections here."

Okay, she was back to bloody square one again. "Then why did we just have a three-legged race to get here?" she demanded again.

On his own power, Joshua had hobbled over to the vehicle. It was less risky making the call from a public place—provided he could find a public place, he thought. He placed his hand on the passenger door and looked at her. "For this."

The vehicle was a truck and at least ten years old. It had seen its share of labor. Joshua covered either side of his eyes and looked in through the window. "Let's hope there's gas in the tank."

"Doesn't do us much good without the keys." The minute she pointed that out, Pru realized that probably wasn't going to be an obstacle for Secret Agent Man. She looked at him. "Or are you one of those men who know how to grab two wires and make the car go?"

He spared her a smile. "Yeah, I'm one of those guys."

Prudence tried the door. Locked. She frowned. "How are you going to get in? You don't have a coat hanger."

Very gently, glancing back at the house to make sure that no one had turned on a light or appeared in the window, Joshua moved her aside. His back was to her and he was doing something with the keyhole. She thought she detected the sound of metal against metal.

"Don't need one," he told her. The next second,

the driver's door was opened. He hit the lock release. "Get in."

She did, then opened the glove compartment. Inside was a jumbled mess, but she found a stub of a pencil and what looked like a faded receipt. Joshua had dragged himself into the driver's seat and was working on the wiring beneath the steering wheel. When he looked up, she was getting out of the truck again.

"Hey," he called after her as loudly as he dared. But she didn't turn around. Instead, she ran to the front door. Stooping down, she placed whatever she'd scribbled down sticking out from beneath the worn mat. The next minute, she came running back just as the old truck rumbled to life.

"What did you do?" he wanted to know, losing no time in driving away.

She settled back. The seat belt on her side, she noticed, was stuck. She gave up trying to use it. "I left a note."

His mouth fell opened. "You did *what?*"

"I left a note," she repeated. "Saying that we'd bring the truck back." In her mind, it was the right thing to do, despite the dire circumstances they found themselves in. What if this was an innocent bystander? They didn't deserve to think that their truck had been stolen. "I didn't want him to worry it was stolen for good."

"And your note is supposed to make this guy feel better?" he asked incredulously. This certainly didn't fit the pattern of Pru the Shrew.

"I said we'd bring it back," she reminded him.

He snorted. "So he's supposed to believe the word of a car thief."

"Car borrower," she corrected vehemently. "And why not?"

Joshua was at a loss for words. He didn't know where to begin to answer that. So he didn't.

Chapter 7

The silence within the cab of the truck surprised him. She'd stopped talking, as if following his lead. At any other time, he would have enjoyed that. But right now, he needed to know something and he was praying for the right answer.

"Did you sign your name to it?" Joshua finally demanded. "The note," he emphasized when she didn't say anything in response immediately. "Did you sign your name to it?"

He didn't realize, until she spoke, that the reason she hadn't answered was because she was fuming. At him. "No, I didn't sign my name to it. How stupid do you think I am?"

He was tempted to answer that, but he had no idea how she would react and he was taking no chances. "Then whoever's truck this is has a promissory note from an anonymous person telling him that his vehicle will be returned. Eventually." He slanted her an incredulous look. "That should comfort him."

Just what was he driving at? "You'd rather I signed it?"

She'd missed the damn point. She'd left fingerprints on the paper. Fingerprints that could be traced. "I'd rather you hadn't done anything at all."

Easy for him to say. The man probably hadn't had a conscience since he was five. She, however, wasn't like that. "I'm not a thief."

He spared her another look and saw that she was genuinely indignant. "No one said you were. Desperate times, desperate measures."

Joshua paused for a moment, easing his foot off the gas. Trying to get his bearings. He knew roughly where he was. Very roughly. They were both exhausted and could do with getting a little rest if not actual sleep. But he wanted to put more miles between them and her captors before he thought about putting his head to a pillow. Making a decision, he pressed gently down on the accelerator again, going due south.

She was being quiet again. There was something eerily unnatural about that. "How are you holding up?" he asked her.

"I've been better," she retorted angrily. And then, because he had asked and because he had saved her, at least to some degree, Pru grudgingly added, "I've also been worse."

He thought he knew what she was referring to. Two seconds before he climbed in through her window. "The image of bondage comes to mind."

"What about you?" she asked, then glanced down at his leg. The material she'd wrapped around it was discolored with blood. This was not good. "You need to have your leg looked at."

"You're taking care of that," he told her glibly. He'd been trained to tough it out, to put his assignment first, his own needs last. There'd be time enough to see to his wound later.

"By someone with a medical degree," Pru emphasized. She nodded at the wound. "That could get infected. Not a pretty sight."

The sincerity of the comment surprised him. Joshua raised his gaze to hers for a split second before looking back at the pea soup before him. "You sound like you've seen it."

"I have," she replied. To avoid any probing looks, she turned her face forward again. "I've seen a lot of things I'd rather not have seen. Things that shouldn't be," she added under her breath.

He nodded, remembering what her dossier had said. "That would be your stint in the Red Cross."

She hated the fact that he knew everything about her and she nothing about him. The few things he'd tossed to her could be a lie, a cover, while he somehow had gotten access to her whole life history.

"Is there *anything* about me you don't know?" Pru wanted to know.

She saw the corner of his mouth curve. "I skimmed over the part about your dress and shoe size," he told her glibly.

She doubted he'd skipped even that. He struck her as the kind of man who wasn't satisfied until he had all the information at his disposal. "To maintain a little mystery?" she quipped.

The slight smile became a full-blown grin. She thought she detected a hint of a dimple in his cheek and tried not to stare. Dimples were endearing, this man was not.

Joshua maintained his expression despite the pain that kept wafting through him, ebbing and flowing and creating odd, electrical little moments where he could literally feel every hair on his head as if it were standing at attention.

"Exactly." He paused, allowing his curiosity to get the better of him. There was nothing else to do but talk and this way, he could get to actually know her and use that to his advantage. "Why'd you do it?" When she looked at him quizzically, he clarified, "Why did you join the Red Cross?"

Why had she joined?

The question echoed in her head. It was something she'd felt she had to do, perhaps to even the balance sheet as her father went deeper and deeper into politics. Not that she actually thought her father was a bad man, he wasn't. But she thought of politics as a less-than-clean undertaking. Politics always seemed to get in the way of getting anything necessary done. It was a game of greed where the winner took all and the loser was forever mired in poverty. Shackled to it.

But she had no intention of explaining herself to this man, or allowing him to try to analyze her motives. So she answered his question with a question of her own, putting him on the spot instead.

"Why did you become a secret agent man?"

Secret Agent Man. It was the title of an old sixties song and the thought of it made him smile. Life had gotten ever so much more complicated than it supposedly was in the sixties.

Or at least so people thought. But human nature being what it was, things had always been complicated on some level.

He shrugged as he made a careful right turn. "You might say I went into the family business."

She took the most logical guess as to who he'd followed. "Father?"

It took everything he had not to laugh out loud. "No."

All right, in this day and age, women served just as much as men. After all, Julia Child had been part of the OSS near the end of the Second World War. Though she couldn't see him in this light, maybe Joshua was closer to his mother and had wanted to cull her favor. "Mother, then?"

He thought of the small, frail woman who these

days had trouble deciding what to have for breakfast. Despite it all, he had a very soft spot in his heart for her. Unlike his father. "Wrong again."

She threw up her hands. "The nanny who seduced you at sixteen."

"Fifteen and she was my French teacher, not my nanny," he informed her matter-of-factly, then grinned, remembering. "And I seduced her. But, no, none of the above." He didn't want her getting close to the truth. "Let's just say it was a member of my family and let it go at that." He turned the tables quickly to keep her from continuing. "Is that why you volunteered with the Red Cross? Because you were following someone's footsteps?"

He knew for a fact that it wasn't, but if he got her talking, maybe she'd forget about her own line of questioning. Besides, getting her to talk helped pass the time as he continued to drive carefully along the fog-devoured road.

Pru blew out a breath. It all seemed so long ago. Just before her father had become prime minister. "Not exactly. I'm atoning for the sins of the father, so to speak."

And what the hell was that supposed to mean? "You really are hard to follow."

From where she sat, it wasn't hard at all. "That's because you're probably accustomed to women who have the brains of single-cell amoebas."

A retort rose to his lips instantly, but he bit it back. "Why do you do that?"

"Do what?" she asked innocently.

She knew damn well what he meant, he thought. "Use insults to push people away."

"Because if I shoved you physically," she said sweetly, "it wouldn't be good sportsmanship since you're wounded." And then she grew serious. "Which brings us full circle to the topic of getting that wound of yours looked at—and don't start that play on words again." She peered out through the windshield, seeing nothing more than she had a moment ago. Fog and more fog. "Isn't there a hospital in this godforsaken area?" For all she could see, they could have been in the heart of a city or in the middle of the country. There was absolutely no indication, one way or another. "Or at least a pharmacy of some sort?"

He saw her point about the hospital, but not about the latter. "What good would that do?"

"Because, Secret Agent Man, pharmacies have disinfectants and bandages and sharp, pointy things I could use to get that bullet out."

The very thought of the woman next to him, wielding a knife near his flesh, brought a cold shiver down his spine. But she was right. He had to get the wound taken care of, and soon, because it could become infected. And an infection, or worse, was most definitely not on his agenda.

He thought for a second, trying to visualize the map he'd studied before coming out here. "I think there's a small hamlet around here somewhere."

A hamlet. God, they were in Shakespeare country. "Where *are* we, anyway?"

"They took you deep into Haworth."

Her eyes widened. He could almost hear it in her voice. "Haworth?" she echoed. That brought to mind moors and incredible desolation. "Just how long was I out?"

This was the first he'd heard that she'd been unconscious, but he could see how her abductors would prefer that. "Not being there, I wouldn't know."

"It was a rhetorical question," Prudence snapped at him.

- She was back in form, he thought. And then he tried to get her to expand on her story for his own information. "They struck you?"

"Yes," she acknowledged grudgingly. It almost felt like a failing on her part, to have allowed that. "Out of anger, I'd imagine."

Joshua pressed his lips together, knowing she wouldn't have appreciated a grin just now. "You're really going to have to learn how not to set people off, Prudence," he told her. "Just what did you say to the guy?"

"Nothing."

"You had to have said something," he insisted.

She shifted in her seat. "One of them hit me in the back of the head after I head-butted one of his partners."

Joshua stopped driving and looked at her. Head-butting. Who would have thought? And then he laughed. "You really are something else." He began to drive again. "What else did you do?"

"Nothing," she insisted, then shrugged. "I bit another one of them."

The woman was a regular wildcat. He was surprised they'd managed to kidnap her at all. "God, I'm glad you're on my side."

"Isn't it the other way around? You were sent to be on my side," she reminded him.

"Yes, I was." And it was nice to know that Pru the Shrew could take care of herself if the occasion called for it.

She'd asked him before, but he hadn't given her an answer she found satisfactory. "Why didn't my father send in more people than just you?"

"We thought less harm would come to you if just one person was sent to quietly penetrate the premises where they were holding you rather than having an army overrun the place."

She would have rather had the army, but she shrugged. "Makes sense, I guess," she murmured.

"But you would have felt safer with an army."

Now there he was wrong, she thought. Dead wrong. "I don't 'feel' safe, Secret Agent Man. Ever. I'm a walking target and I know it."

Well, if she felt that way, why was she behaving like a petulant child about it? "Then why don't you let your father appoint a bodyguard?"

He might as well have been talking about prison. "Because I want to live my life, not have someone censoring my every move, telling me what I can or can't do. And I like to jog alone," she emphasized, "not with an overseer."

"Well, that certainly worked out well for you."

She frowned at the sarcasm in his voice. Frowned more at the fact that he was right.

"Shouldn't you have found someplace by now? They call it Great Britain, but it's really not that big a country," she insisted.

And just as she made her demand, she saw what appeared to look like streetlights piercing the thick clouds up ahead.

Joshua gestured at the horizon. "Ask and ye shall receive."

There he went, acting as if he was some kind of deity. "Took you long enough," she muttered.

Joshua nodded in her direction as he drove toward the lights. "You're welcome."

The lights turned out to be those coming through the windows of another farmhouse. But this one was nothing like the one where she'd been held captive. This farmhouse was two-storied and looked very modern and well taken care of. It was more in keeping with something one of her father's friends might have used as a vacation home to get away from the pressures of government work.

Pru looked at her wounded rescuer uncertainly. "Have you been driving around in circles?"

He knew what she was thinking. That somehow they'd happened upon another farmhouse in the cottage's vicinity. But that wasn't the case. Even in a fog, he had a keen sense of direction when it came to traveling. "No. Due south."

She cocked her head, studying the building. "You're sure?"

There was no hesitation in his voice, nor, surprisingly, any indication that he found her question insulting. "I'm sure."

Pru found herself believing him. "All right then." She put her hand on the door handle and tugged it open. The fine mist that had been falling was turning into rain again. "Wait here."

"The hell I will," he snapped. He was responsible for her. There was no way he was about to let her just waltz over to a house he hadn't had time to scout out yet.

As he stumbled out of the truck, he looked down at his cell phone. Still no signal. Or maybe it had been damaged in the car wreck. He cursed under his breath.

Pru thought the choice words were aimed at her because she'd told him to stay in the truck. She gave him an exasperated look. "I bet you made your mother's hair turn gray."

His mother had been getting her hair color from a bottle with the aid of a hairstylist for as long as he could remember. "My father did that to her years before I had a chance."

Until he'd broken out of his shell at the ripe age of fifteen, Joshua had tried to be a model son. It was his way of attempting to compensate for his father's behavior. His mother took no notice and he watched her slowly slip into a fantasy world, choosing to ignore what was in front of her.

Prudence Hill would have had no patience with a woman like his mother, he thought.

Pru picked up something in his tone as they began to make their way to the front door. "Sounds like you and your father don't get along."

She was perceptive, he'd give her that. A little too perceptive. And damned annoying because of it. "Maybe you'd like to apply to the agency after I get you back."

The look she gave him said she'd caught him in a lie. "I thought you said earlier that you didn't belong to an agency."

"No," he corrected, "I said that I didn't belong to any of the ones you mentioned. We're here," he pointed out.

"So we are." Removing his arm from her shoulder, she took a breath and rang the bell. The first few bars of *God Save the Queen* chimed, disturbing the stillness of the night.

A few moments later, the front door opened and an older looking gentleman with tufts of white hair surrounding his perfectly round head like a halo looked them over in utter silence. Eyes as blue as cobalt washed over first her, then Joshua. Whatever conclusion he came to he kept to himself.

"My friend's been hurt," Pru told him, taking the initiative and talking quickly like a distraught woman. "I was wondering if perhaps you might be able to spare a few bandages, some peroxide—and a needle and thread," she added for good measure.

The strange little man finally spoke, asking, "You a doctor?"

"Nurse," she responded without blinking an eye. She could feel Joshua staring at her but she didn't dare look in his direction.

The man pursed his lips, looking over the length of his visitor until his eyes came to rest on the wound. He pointed one slightly crooked finger at it. "What kind of a wound is that one?"

"A bad one," Pru responded, then, her mind racing, she added, "He was gored by a goat. Made a neat, round hole in him, didn't it?" she asked as if it was something to be pondered over and displayed.

White eyebrows drew together in a wiggly, perplexed line. "McCaffrey's goat?"

Good, she'd taken a chance since this was farm country that *someone* had a goat. "He didn't stop to introduce himself, I'm afraid," she answered amiably, smiling at the man. "We were out for a drive this afternoon when we got lost." She leaned in closer to the man. "You know how you gentlemen hate to ask for directions."

"Wasn't anyone to ask," Joshua chimed in, playing along.

"There was when we started out," she told him with a smile that was a tad too wide. Joshua had no idea what to make of it, but he was willing to follow her lead if it ultimately resulted in food and shelter.

There was the sound of shuffling in the background and the next moment, a rosy looking woman joined them, elbowing aside the old man who was half a head shorter than she was. She looked at her visitors with curiosity. "Who's this, Alvin?"

Alvin's voice lowered to a grudgingly subservient level. "I didn't get a name."

"Ophelia," Prudence said, putting her hand out to the woman. "Ophelia Lawrence. And this is my husband—" she nodded toward Joshua "—James."

"Husband?" the old man echoed. "I thought you said he was your friend."

"He is." Pru deliberately addressed her words to the woman. "Aren't you friends with your husband?"

"Dearie, I don't even want to talk to my husband half the time, much less be friends with him. Step out of the way, Alvin," she ordered, taking charge. "Can't you see the young man's hurt? Or is it your intent to have him bleed to death in our doorway?"

"No, no, of course not." Alvin quickly backed out of the way.

"Well, help her," his wife dictated. She made an exasperated face at her husband, then looked at her guest. "Honestly. Men. Don't have the sense they were born with. Elizabeth Wakefield," she added, and offered her hand.

"I've often thought that," Pru agreed, shaking hands then sending a backward glance toward

Joshua as the older man took her place and laced Joshua's arm across his own bent shoulders.

Joshua offered the older man an encouraging smile as he allowed himself to be taken into the dimly lit house, hoping he wasn't making a deadly mistake.

Chapter 8

The moment he was inside, Joshua looked around. The lights overhead were flickering like a flirtatious, overzealous femme fatale. The uneven light was distracting as he searched for the one thing he needed at the moment. Unable to locate it, he turned toward Alvin as the older man awkwardly lowered him onto a chair in the kitchen.

"Do you have a telephone?" Joshua asked.

It was Elizabeth who answered before her husband had a chance. "Yes, we've got one."

Joshua wondered if the woman made no follow-up offer because she thought he was going to make a costly call. Wherever the phone was, it wasn't in the kitchen. "Would you mind if I used it?"

To his surprise, Elizabeth chuckled, amused. "Well, I don't mind, but you might."

Joshua glanced toward Pru but she didn't seem any more enlightened than he did. "Excuse me?"

Elizabeth crossed to a room just beyond the kitchen. From the sound of a medicine cabinet being closed, Joshua surmised it was the bathroom.

"He's a polite one, isn't he, Alvin?" She returned with supplies in her arms. "You'd mind because you'd be getting frustrated, trying to make a call." She deposited bandages and gauze pads on the table. "Phone's been dead since this storm started." She crossed her arms before her ample chest. "Happens a lot out here. Don't get much regular service every time Mother Nature throws a fit. But we don't mind." She shrugged carelessly, looking toward her husband. "Don't have anyone to call anyway."

He had to get in touch with the prime minister, or at least his own people, who could then get in contact with Hill. "How far away is the nearest town?"

This time, it was Alvin who fielded the question. He avoided looking at his wife as he answered, "Far enough to make the trip interesting. Close enough to get to if we need anything. Why?"

There was no harm in being truthful—up to a point. "I really need to make that call."

Alvin nodded as his wife stepped out of the room again. "Then your best bet is to keep on going. Service isn't all that good at Spurn Head. Better to go on to the next town. It's about twenty kilometers from here." Just as he said it, the lights began to give up the ghost. It was clear that there was a power failure in the making. "They don't lose their electricity when the storms come."

"Alvin, get some more candles for these nice people," Elizabeth instructed as she began lighting the various candles that had already been placed around the room. They looked like so many mushrooms randomly sprouting after the rain. "We keep these out," she explained to Pru. "Never know when you might need them. Now—" she placed her hands on her ample hips "—what else did you say you needed?"

Pru pressed her lips together. She wasn't looking forward to what she had to do, but if she didn't do something, there was no telling what could happen to Lazlo's leg. "A needle, thread, a sharp knife and some peroxide."

Elizabeth nodded at the mention of the first three, but she shook it at the last item. "Don't have any of that. But I've got alcohol. The rubbing kind," she emphasized. "I don't abide any of the other being around," she confessed. "Makes a man's head fuzzy and Alvin's is fuzzy enough as it is. On the inside," she added with a chuckle when Pru glanced in the old man's direction and looked at his tufts of white hair.

Even as she spoke, Elizabeth was busy gathering the items together, fetching the knife from a drawer in the kitchen, the needle and thread from another closet, then stepping back into the bathroom. Alvin, meanwhile, was spreading more candles around the kitchen.

Pru looked at Joshua. He was still sitting on the chair where Alvin had deposited him, looking a little pale, even with only the light from the candles illuminating the room.

"Too bad about the alcohol," Pru said to Joshua, lowering her voice. "I have a feeling you might need some."

Joshua looked down at his thigh. It was throbbing like a son of a gun and despite the makeshift bandage, it was still oozing blood. "All depends on how good you are."

Elizabeth handed her a large bottle of rubbing alcohol. "Well, we'll just have to see about that, won't we?" Pru said, bracing herself. Her tongue felt as if it was sticking to the roof of her mouth.

Time to get busy, she told herself, placing the bottle of alcohol on the table and picking up the knife. She carefully pierced the leg of Joshua's pants, then quickly ran the blade through it, slitting the material down to the cuff.

Startled, Joshua stared at her. "What are you doing?"

She would have thought that was obvious. "I have to cut away the material to get at the wound."

Joshua leaned into her so that neither of the two other people in the room could hear him. "First I sacrifice my shirt, now this? I usually know a woman more than a few hours before I get naked in front of her."

"First time for everything," Pru whispered back

glibly. She tried not to let the image he'd just painted in her mind distract her. It was bad enough that the man had a chest you could bounce coins on, she didn't want her thoughts getting carried away about the rest of him.

Out of the corner of her eye, Pru saw Elizabeth leave the room. Probably couldn't stomach the sight of blood, she guessed. Not that she could blame the woman. She wasn't exactly all that keen on this herself, but the alternative wasn't very promising and whether she'd asked him to or not, Lazlo *had* come to her aid. The way she saw it, even though she wouldn't have said anything to him about it, she owed him.

With the pant leg sufficiently out of the way, picking up the alcohol Pru walked over to the sink and disinfected the knife before crossing back to Joshua. She poised the tip of the knife over the wound.

"Ready?"

Maybe a little alcohol might have been welcome right about now, Joshua thought. Braced, he nodded. "Ready. Get it over with."

Pru ran the tip of her tongue along her lower lip, worried. If Lazlo jerked involuntarily, or moved, she might accidentally cut him deeper than she intended. She looked at Alvin. "Maybe you'd better put your hands on his shoulders, hold him down for me if you don't mind."

Alvin nodded nervously. But as the old man was about to do as she asked, Joshua waved him back and looked into her eyes. She saw the agent's steely resolve. "No need," he told her. "Just do it."

Pru took a deep breath and willed her hand to remain steady. Then she cut into the wound as quickly as possible. After what seemed like an interminable amount of probing, she was rewarded with the faint sound of metal on metal. She'd located the bullet with the tip of the filleting knife that Elizabeth had given her. Now all she had to do was dig it out.

All.

Throughout the short procedure, she kept glancing up at Joshua to see how he was holding up. To her surprise, he neither flinched nor moved a muscle. If it weren't for the feel of his flesh, she would have said she was cutting into a stone statue.

And then the bullet was out. "There's the little bugger," she announced with triumph, putting it on the table in front of Joshua. She took the knife and put it in the sink, then washed her hands again.

"So," Alvin said thoughtfully, looking from one to the other. It was obvious that, for the time being, he'd decided to let this pass. "Always was an ornery animal," he commented.

She'd forgotten about the "goat." She pressed her lips together. "Armed to the teeth, he was," she quipped.

She breathed a sigh of relief. "Part two," Pru announced, returning to Joshua. Threading the needle, she disinfected both it and the thread. She got down on her knees and then carefully pierced Joshua's skin as she began stitching up the wound.

It took only five stitches. Pru held her breath as she took each stitch and pulled it through. The only audible sound was Alvin, breathing. There seemed to be nothing coming from Lazlo, not even one cleanly drawn breath.

The man was a robot, she thought, amazed and a little unnerved.

Finished, Pru put down the needle and thread, feeling considerably more shaken inside than she judged Joshua was. She dropped into the chair opposite him. She didn't bother hiding her amazement. "You take pain like a warrior."

He raised a shoulder and let it drop, dismissing the praise. "Didn't see the point in yelling in your ear and if I moved, who knows what you would have cut or stitched."

She laughed at that, getting a clear image of just what part he was referring to. And then she noticed that Lazlo was just now uncurling his fingers from either side of the chair. Looked like he'd been holding on to the entire time she'd worked on him. She couldn't help wondering—if she flipped the chair over, would there be a deep impression of his fingerprints?

"Very true," she agreed.

Elizabeth popped her head in the doorway. "Surgery over?" she wanted to know.

"All done," Pru told her. Rising, she turned toward

the sink to wash her hands for a third time. As she moved she felt stiff. Was that due to her own nerves, or the less-than-gentle way she'd been handled these last two days? In either case, she felt sore.

"Then you could stand to use these." Elizabeth placed a folded shirt and pair of pants on the table in front of Joshua. "Keep you from running around the countryside, looking like some half-naked Tarzan character. They belonged to our boy, Nathan," she explained, patting the small pile. "He was about your height and size when he was taken from us. We've still got a bunch of his clothes."

Pru stopped drying her hands and crossed over to the other woman. She put her arms around her, feeling genuine sympathy. "Oh, I'm so sorry."

"Yes." Elizabeth sighed heavily. "So am I." She glanced at Alvin. "We," she amended. "But these things happen, I suppose." And then she added with a hopeful smile, "Maybe someday he'll come back."

Pru exchanged glances with Joshua. That wasn't exactly possible. "I'm afraid I don't understand."

Elizabeth pursed her lips, shaking her head. "Neither do we. Why he'd run off with that two-bit tart is simply beyond me. Raised him up to be God-fearing and decent and the minute he turned twenty-one, he ran off with the first little tart who smiled at him." She stopped when she saw the puzzled looks on their faces. "What's the matter?"

"You said he was taken from you," Joshua reminded her.

"Well, he was," Elizabeth insisted. "By *her.*" The single word sounded damning. She huffed, shaking her head, obviously pushing away the unpleasant memory. "It's getting late and you two must be tired after your big adventure." She tittered slightly. "With the goat." And then her expression softened into an inviting smile. "You can stay the night if you like. Have our boy's old room. Bed's kinda small, but it's better than sleeping in a truck I'd wager."

"You're being very kind," Joshua told her, taking out his wallet.

But as he began to take out a few bills, the woman pushed his hand aside. There was almost indignation in her eyes.

"Put that away, I didn't ask you for money now, did I?" She eyed the wallet until Joshua finally slipped it back into what was left of his pants. "That's what's wrong with the world these days, people have completely forgotten about common hospitality."

"Well, you obviously haven't," Pru told her, giving the woman a warm, heartfelt hug. She felt empathy stirring inside her, enough to bring tears to her eyes. With effort, Pru willed them back, blinking to keep them from spilling. "Thank you."

"Go on with you." Clearing her throat, Elizabeth waved the two of them off. "Alvin will show you to Nathan's room. Might be a mite dusty," she apologized as they turned to go. "I haven't been in there since he left."

Pru gave the woman's hand a squeeze, letting her know that she understood. Turning, she offered her shoulder to Joshua for him to lean on.

The corners of his mouth curved slightly. "This is getting to be a habit," he commented.

"Well, just don't get used to it," she warned him, threading her arm around his waist. Silently, she gave herself the same warning.

Mercifully, Nathan's room was on the first floor, which meant that Joshua didn't have to climb any stairs.

When Alvin brought them to it, the older man paused in the doorway as they walked into the room. "Will you be needing anything else?"

Joshua hesitated for a second. Asking felt like an imposition, but he wasn't thinking of himself. This was for the woman the agency was being paid handsomely to have him retrieve and protect. So he asked.

"Could you spare a bite to eat? P—" Joshua stopped himself just in time. He was about to use her name, which was *not* the one she'd given the older couple. He couldn't remember what she'd called herself, so he used a neutral term. "My wife hasn't had anything to eat today and I know she's starving."

Alvin nodded his head vigorously. "Got lots of shepherd's pie left from dinner. Elizabeth always makes too much." He looked apologetic. "But you'll have to have it cold, what with the stove out because of the electricity and all."

"Right now," Pru confessed, "I wouldn't care if it was frozen."

Alvin looked as if he believed her. Which prompted him to hurry. "Be back in a second," he promised, shuffling away as quickly as he could.

Pru turned away from the doorway and looked at Joshua. He was standing behind her. The room felt rather small. "That was very thoughtful of you."

Joshua shrugged. "I have my moments."

Her mouth curved. Maybe she'd been too hasty to judge him. Her life had always been filled with people whose allegiance was strictly to her father and to his position, whatever it was at the time. She had to admit she liked being placed first for a change.

"Apparently."

Joshua tried to take a step. It wasn't easy but he was determined. He glanced down at the freshly bandaged thigh. "You know, when you told that woman you were a nurse, I thought you were kidding."

"I was," she countered. Digging out the bullet and then closing up the wound was something she'd learned while working in the various poverty-infested countries while serving with the Red Cross. "But telling her that saved time," she explained. "Elizabeth would have wanted to hear details about how I learned to do what I did otherwise." She smiled up at him, thinking that he really did have beautiful eyes for a secret agent. "Besides, I have a feeling you'd feel better if I didn't go around telling people who I really was."

She was right and he was relieved that she understood that without his having to tell her. It would have come across as too much of a lecture, something, he had a hunch, she would have highly resented.

"Intuitive, handy and beautiful." His appreciative smile deepened. "Quite a combination."

There was something about that smile that pulled a woman in, Pru thought, trying to be analytical rather than affected. She turned her face up to his. "Are you coming on to me, Secret Agent Man?"

Another time, another place…he couldn't help thinking. But out loud, he told her, "It's against the rules."

She didn't move back, didn't draw away. "And you always follow rules."

Damn, but for two cents, he'd like to see what it felt like kissing that sarcastic mouth. "Yes."

Pru drew closer to him, so close that he could feel each word along his skin the second she uttered it. "Always?" she repeated.

He should be putting some space between them. There really were rules to follow and none of them allowed for what he was thinking now.

"Always."

Pru raised herself up on the toes of her sneakers, never taking her eyes off him. Her lips were less than a fraction away from his. As she spoke, her mouth came within a hairbreadth of touching his.

"Really?"

There was amusement dripping from every letter. And then, to test his resolve and her theory, that he was the kind who easily bent rules if it suited him, Pru brought her mouth to his.

Because he was confident that he wasn't about to lose his head just because Pru the Shrew had also turned out to be a tease, Joshua didn't move his head back and try to avoid what he knew was about to happen. Instead, he decided to teach her a lesson. That there were consequences for playing with fire. He not only didn't move his head, he kissed her back.

Taking firm hold of her shoulders, he immediately deepened the kiss.

And then deepened it some more.

The next thing Joshua knew, he was framing her face with his hands and there was this wild, heady pumping of blood going on in his veins. So wild and so loud that it blocked out everything.

Everything but the heat from her mouth and the heat from his own body. Especially since it was now pressed urgently against hers. He was absorbing every point of contact. Whether this latest twist was of his doing or hers he couldn't swear to with certainty, but all he knew for a fact was that there wasn't enough space between them for a moonbeam to squeeze through.

And he was enjoying it.

One second she was teasing him, having a little fun at his expense, the next, the electrical storm they had previously been subjected to had now moved into the four walls of this tiny, drab bedroom.

Not only into the bedroom, but into her veins as well.

Pru could hardly breathe, much less think. But she could react. Oh, Lord, could she ever react.

And she did.

Almost involuntarily, Pru had brought her body to his, sealing herself to him as closely as her mouth was sealed to his lips.

And then there was this noise, this uncomfortable, embarrassed noise. Focusing, Pru realized that someone was clearing his throat.

Alvin.

Pru jerked her head back, away from Joshua, and turned toward the doorway. Good as his word, Elizabeth's husband had returned. He was holding a small tray in his hands.

More like clutching it, actually. On the tray were two plates of what looked like mashed potatoes with bits of meat and several peas peering out from beneath it.

"Didn't mean to interrupt," he apologized, tending the apology to the slates on the wooden floor.

"You weren't interrupting," Pru told him. She tried to keep her tone matter-of-fact as she took the tray from him, then set it down on the small bureau. "This is more than generous," she told him, offering him a wide smile. "Thank you."

Alvin nodded, then looked at Joshua. He seemed to be more comfortable talking to his own gender. "Brought you something else." As he spoke, he looked over his shoulder. There was no one there, and he offered the "something else" to Joshua. "But from the looks of it, you might not need this to take the edge off." He chuckled to himself as he handed over a half-consumed pint of whiskey.

Joshua refrained from taking the bottle. "I thought your wife said she doesn't keep spirits in the house."

"She doesn't. Doesn't mean that I can't." Alvin winked broadly at both of them.

Joshua shook his head. "I can't take this from you," he protested.

But Alvin took the bottle and placed it in his guest's hand. "Sure you can. Not like there's not more hidden about, here and there. Like I said—" again he glanced over his shoulder "—it takes the edge off." Stepping back, he put his hand on the doorknob. "You two have a good night of it. Need anything else, just yell out." His eyes went from one to the other. "Though I don't think you'll be yelling for me if you do." Again, Alvin winked broadly, an impish smile on his lips. "Ah, to be young just one more time," he murmured as he left. "And free."

The words trailed out after him.

Joshua hobbled over to the door and flipped the lock on it. "Nice old man," he commented.

Pru didn't answer. The second the door had

closed, she turned toward the tray and gave her full attention to one of the plates of shepherd's pie. Her mother had taught her never to talk with her mouth full.

Chapter 9

Joshua smiled to himself. The women he was accustomed to were obsessively weight conscious. Even his own mother worried about the extra ounce or two she occasionally put on. The prime minister's daughter ate as if she truly enjoyed food, even taking into account the fact that she was probably starving.

Pru raised her eyes from the plate. Secret Agent Man was watching her. She could almost read his mind. She shrugged as she swallowed the last bit in her mouth. "I guess I didn't realize how hungry I was until I started eating," she confessed. "My stomach feels as if it was glued to my spine."

He picked up his plate from the tray and slid half of what was there onto hers. "In that case, have some of mine."

Not that she didn't welcome the extra portion, but she didn't want to seem gluttonous. "And what are you going to live on? Air?"

Settling back on the bed beside her, he sank his fork into the serving that was left. "I've eaten today. From what I could piece together, you haven't eaten much in the past two days. Those guys back there didn't seem like the hospitable type," he said before he began to eat.

She'd had exactly one meal since this whole ordeal had started. "All right, I'm not going to argue with you."

He was about to say that was a first. But the words faded from his lips as he watched her slip the forkful of food between her lips. Pru closed her eyes, apparently savoring this mouthful just as much as she had the very first. She looked as if she was in ecstasy.

It made him wonder if she looked nearly that enthused and passionate when she was making love with a man.

The moment the thought came into his head, he discarded it. None of his concern, he told himself. The only thing that *was* his concern was getting her back to London and her father before the vote was taken on Wednesday.

Mentally crossing his fingers, he put his plate back on the bureau and took out his cell phone. But when he tried to make a call, nothing happened. Again.

Snapping the cell phone shut, Joshua muttered a few choice words under his breath. It was beginning to look as if the only way to get in touch with the prime minister was going to be to physically show up at Number 10 Downing Street.

He had a little more than fifteen hours to bring her back safely. Piece of cake, he told himself.

Pru reached for the glass of water Alvin had brought her. "Still no signal?"

"Nothing." Joshua seriously thought about taking a long swig from the half-pint that the old man had left with him, but it was only the frustration urging him on. He couldn't drink on the job, no matter what so-called glamorous spy stories maintained to the contrary.

Picking up his plate again, he resumed eating. Prudence was looking at him. Probably wondering if she could ask for more, he thought.

But when she spoke, it had nothing to do with sharing his dinner. "This probably won't do any good, but you could try making a call from mine."

Joshua stopped eating. "You have a cell phone?" Each word was metered out and wrapped in disbelief.

Why was he looking at her so oddly? "Yes."

She had to be kidding, he thought. "The kidnappers didn't take your cell phone away?"

Her plate empty, she stood up and placed it on the bureau, then dug a phone out of the inner pocket of her jogging shorts. The cell phone was one of the smallest he'd ever seen.

Pru held it up for his benefit. "Apparently not. Maybe they didn't think they had to worry since they had me completely bound and gagged. And since yours isn't working, I figured mine won't, either."

Crossing to her, Joshua took the phone from Pru. He didn't care how tied up she was, the kidnappers wouldn't have overlooked searching her to make sure she didn't have anything to help her get away. That most definitely included a cell phone.

"Something's not adding up here," he told her. Flipping the cell open, he pressed the green button to activate the phone line. He stared at the screen. Nothing.

Pru sighed, frustrated. There had to be some way to get in touch with her father. She didn't want him worrying on her account. Or going against his conscience because he thought that was the only way to save her. "Doesn't work either, I take it."

She saw him raise an eyebrow as he looked the phone over carefully. "Not sure about that yet."

"What do you mean?" The next minute, he was taking the phone apart. "Be careful," she warned. "That's expensive."

"Not without a battery," he told her.

"Then what's that?" she wanted to know, pointing to the gray rectangular devise that was inside her phone.

"Not like any battery I've ever seen," he answered. Taking it out, he examined it slowly. Lighter than a standard cell phone battery, it felt almost hollow. He turned it over and then stiffened. "We have to get out of here."

She didn't understand. All she wanted to do was stretch out on the bed and fall asleep. "Why?" she protested. "We're safe here."

"No, we're not," he told her firmly.

He had a job to do, she understood that. But no one knew they were here. What was the point of fleeing? At least until morning.

When she spoke, it was as if she was trying to reason with and calm a willful, stubborn child. "I understand that you're programmed to worry, but I am not about to let paranoia govern my every move. I'm tired, Secret Agent Man. We're both tired, you probably even more than me. If you want, I'll even take the first watch so that you can—"

Instead of trying to outtalk her, Joshua merely held up what she still thought was supposed to be the battery. What did that prove?

"Yes, so?" And then she realized that there was a tracking device within all the later model cell phones. Like hers. But she also knew the phone had to be on, sending out a signal and there *were* no signals going out. He *knew* that, she thought. "If those thugs back at the farmhouse think they're going to use the GPS device on it to find me, the signal has to be coming in and as we damn well know, there *is* no signal."

His expression did not change. "No *phone* signal," Joshua emphasized.

"Right, no phone signal." Since he seemed to still be offering the battery to her, she took it. Turning it over in her hand, she looked the so-called light-weight battery from front to back.

And then she saw it.

The tiniest little black dot on the underside. At first, she thought it was just a mark, a tiny piece of dirt that had gotten into her phone. And then she had a sinking sensation in the pit of her stomach.

Pru raised her eyes to Joshua's. "This isn't dirt, is it?"

Joshua took the battery back. Placing it on the floor, black dot exposed, he took the bottle of whiskey and poured some over it. A barely perceptible sizzling sound was emitted for less than a second before it stopped.

"No," he answered, disgusted, "it's not. They're tracking you."

How was that possible? "But signals are out because of the storm."

"Regular signals," he pointed out, hitting his heel against the gray shell just in case. He heard it crack as he ground it against the floor. "Whoever's behind this undoubtedly has access to the latest high-tech devices. That means that this storm probably isn't impeding them in the slightest."

As he spoke, Joshua stripped off his shredded pants and quickly put on the jeans and shirt Elizabeth had brought him. Pru realized that not only was she staring at what probably was the most spectacular specimen of manhood she'd seen in a very long time, but she'd stopped breathing as well. She forced air into her lungs slowly. Apparently his organization required its agents to be in absolute top physical form.

Joshua saw the look on her face and despite the dire circumstances, he made no effort to hide the smile that rose to his lips. "Didn't your mother teach you not to stare, Prudence?"

She swallowed, embarrassed. Hoping that color didn't creep up along her cheeks and give him further satisfaction. "Didn't yours teach you to change your clothes in private?"

"We never got around to talking about that," he quipped dryly. "C'mon, we don't have any time to spare."

But she cast one last longing glance at the bed. "You really think—?"

"I really think," he answered with conviction, not bothering to finish the statement because they both knew what he was saying. That even now, her kidnappers might be closing in on them. Grabbing her hand, he pulled her out of the room.

The house was dark inside. Alvin must have put out the candles. She looked toward the staircase. "Shouldn't we say something to the Wakefields?"

"The less they know, the better off they are," Joshua assured her as he hurried her out the back door.

The air was heavy and pregnant with moisture as the rain remained being held in abeyance. Thunder rumbled in the distance, in between flashes of lightning. Joshua kept his arm out behind him, making sure that she was all but pressed flat against the house as she made her way out in his wake.

She didn't understand why they hadn't gone out the front door. "The car's parked out in front," she protested in an urgent whisper. "Why are we taking the long way around?"

"Precautions," was all he told her.

"Do you really think—?"

Pru's whispered question was abruptly aborted as she caught her breath. The next moment, she was being pushed even farther back into the shadows. Joshua was shielding her with his body as he backed up, dragging her away from the front of the house.

"That's them," she hissed.

Yes, he thought, it was "them." The two men from the farmhouse. The one who'd gone with him to see about his car and the man who'd ordered him to do it. Abandoning their car, they were quickly making their way to the front door.

Joshua blamed himself for the way things were playing out.

"I should have searched you," he muttered under his breath. The sound of breaking glass from the front punctuated his words. "Damn it, I should have known."

Pru willed herself to get a grip. Nothing was going to happen to her. She was going to be all right, she silently promised herself.

"I thought you said you disabled their cars." It came out like an accusation.

"Someone obviously knew how to override what I did," he retorted angrily. His mind raced, trying to make the best of the situation. The kidnappers' car was obviously in better condition than the truck they'd stolen. It made sense to take that one. Even if the keys weren't in the ignition.

He turned toward Pru. "On my count, we make a run for it to the front. When you get there, get into their car. They'll be busy inside. We can get away before they know what's happened."

To his surprise, Pru shook her head and gave no indication that she was going to move an inch no matter how high he counted. "No."

"No?" he echoed incredulously. Had fear frozen her? "What do you mean, no?"

How could he even ask? Didn't he realize what was happening only a few feet away? "We can't just leave and let those thugs torture these people. Who knows what they're liable to do to Alvin and Elizabeth."

She had to pick now to get a heart, he thought angrily. He grabbed her wrist as she began to move to the front door.

"Look," he began impatiently, debating just throwing her over his shoulder and making a run for it, bad leg and all. "I don't like leaving them any more than you do, but they're not my concern, you are."

"Okay." Pru yanked free, then stepped back quickly, holding her hands up out of reach "Then you'll help me help them."

"Damn it, woman." He shook his head, then grabbed her again before she could get away. "All right," he whispered harshly against her ear, bringing her close to him to ensure that she wouldn't make a break for it and do something stupid. Like get herself killed. "But *you* follow *my* lead," he emphasized fiercely. "Otherwise, no deal."

"Fine. Then lead," she told him.

Joshua struggled for patience. This woman was quickly becoming the most annoying assignment he'd had in a long time. If he wasn't careful, she was going to get both of them killed.

"Maybe I should have followed my father into *his* line of work," he muttered.

She looked at him sharply. "What does your father do?"

"Womanize," Joshua retorted.

She didn't know if he was kidding or not, but now wasn't the time to ask.

As they came around the front, he braced himself, ready for anything, knowing that at a moment's notice, he might be forced to give up his life to protect hers. Adrenaline pumped through his veins at an accelerated rate.

He quickly took in the surrounding area. The front door of the Wakefields' house was wide open. There were shards of glass all over the front step. Looking toward the driveway, he saw the car that the kidnappers had to have used. It was empty. Which meant that both kidnappers were now inside, focusing their collective attention on the two old people who were still there.

They heard whimpering. Elizabeth was crying. Pru squeezed his arm urgently. When he looked at her, she begged, "Do something."

Joshua indicated that she should stay behind, or at least walk behind him. She pressed her lips together in a look of frustration, but she nodded. Only then did he enter the house. He measured his steps cautiously, moving to the sound of the voices, ever alert for someone to suddenly come at him from the shadows.

"Don't hurt him," Elizabeth pleaded with someone. There was the sound of flesh meeting flesh and Alvin groaned as Elizabeth screamed. "Please don't hurt him," she begged again.

They were in the kitchen. The Wakefields in their bedclothes, clearly confused and frightened by this invasion. There were two men, dressed in black as if they meant to live in shadows when they weren't torturing people. Pru recognized them immediately.

"Then tell us where they are," the man who'd been the driver of the van that had been used to abduct her ordered. He lowered his gun, holding it over Alvin's left hand and aiming at one of the fingers. The other man was holding Alvin down, flattening the man on the table. The driver spared a glance at the trembling Elizabeth. "Your man's going to lose a digit for each second that you don't tell me."

"They were in the room," Elizabeth cried helplessly. "I saw them there before I went to bed. I don't know where they've gone."

"Looking for me?" Joshua asked calmly. He walked into the kitchen as if he'd come intent on nothing more dangerous than a midnight snack.

When the driver swung around to face him, Joshua fired a single shot. The kidnapper was dead before he hit the floor. Elizabeth screamed, as did Alvin. The second kidnapper reacted instantly, raising his gun. He never got the chance to fire. Pru dove for his midsection, knocking him down.

Joshua was at her side immediately, grabbing the man and yanking him to his feet. "Rope, I need rope," he ordered.

Relieved to have all his fingers still attached, Alvin jumped to his feet and ran to the utility drawer to comply.

"Are you all right?" Joshua asked Elizabeth over the sound of his hostage's curses as he twisted the man's arm behind his back.

"Oh yes, thank you," Elizabeth sobbed. As Alvin passed her with the rope, she clung to him, sobbing with relief that he was all right.

"I'm fine, too. Thanks for asking," Pru ground out

between her teeth as she rose to her feet. With a sigh, she dusted herself off.

"Oh, you're more than fine, dear. You were wonderful," Elizabeth cried.

The expression on Joshua's face was dark. "I told you to stay behind me," he reminded her.

Didn't the man know the meaning of the words *thank you?* "I stopped him," she said indignantly. "He was going to shoot you."

"Not before I shot him," Joshua assured her. He'd been about to fire when he saw Prudence making a dive for the man. He couldn't fire then, not without risking shooting her.

"You're that fast," Pru mocked.

"I'm that fast," he replied without any fanfare. He took the hemp that Alvin had found and began tying up the second kidnapper.

Elizabeth looked from one to the other, her expression mirroring her confusion. She stepped out of the way as Joshua planted the man who had held her husband down onto a chair. "You're not a young married couple, are you?"

"No," Pru replied gently, "we're not." And then she glared at the man Joshua was tying up. If she'd had a gun, she would have shot him herself. Not for abducting her, but for threatening the old couple the way he had. "Didn't they even tell you who they were looking for?" she asked Elizabeth.

Alvin shook his head. "They just kept yelling 'Where are they? Where are they?' We didn't know who they were talking about. You were the only ones who were here, but you didn't look like the type to know people like this."

"We don't," Joshua bit off, giving the ropes a hard yank to make sure they were in place.

"Oh, Alvin, you're bleeding," Elizabeth cried, horrified.

The old man touched the side of his head, then looked down at his fingers. There was bright red blood on them. "So I am."

Pru took charge. "I can take care of that for you," she told Alvin. "I'll be needing that alcohol again, Mrs. Wakefield."

"It's Elizabeth, dear. And what shall I call you?" she asked, turning around in the doorway that led to the bathroom.

"Pru." Pru paused a second, debating. She didn't bother looking toward Joshua for permission. It was her name and her life. "Prudence. Prudence Hill," she finally said.

"Hill." Wiry tufts of white and gray eyebrows drew together. Alvin peered up at her face. "Like the prime minister?"

Pru nodded, then smiled. "Exactly like the prime minister. I'm his daughter. And these two men—" she nodded toward the dead man on the floor and the one that Joshua had just finished tying up "—kidnapped me yesterday morning."

Alcohol in hand, Elizabeth turned toward Joshua. "And you are?"

"The man who rescued her," Joshua replied.

Nonetheless, Elizabeth sighed as she looked from one to the other. "How very romantic."

Alvin clucked his tongue against the roof of his mouth. "Only you would say something like that, Lizzie, with a dead man on our floor." He winced slightly, then clenched his hands in his lap as Pru finished cleaning up his wound. "Speaking of which—" he tried to turn to look at Joshua "—what do we do with him?"

Joshua knew what he would have liked to have done with him—strung him up by his heels as warning to whoever it was who'd sent the kidnapper—but he had a job to complete and vengeance was for those who had time. "Do you have a constable or police officer in town?"

"There's only Jeremy," Alvin told him. "Jeremy Kemp. His range is tracking down stolen bicycles and finding lost dogs. We don't have any real crime here," Alvin confided.

"We've stumbled onto Brigadoon," Joshua commented under his breath, exchanging glances with Pru. "Well, I'm afraid you do now. Do you feel up to going and fetching Jeremy, Mr. Wakefield? He might be more willing to come in the middle of the night if he sees a familiar face. I'll stay here with your wife and Prudence, and see what I can get out of this one—" he nodded toward the bound man "—while you're gone."

"Of course, of course." Alvin stopped a moment

to look at Pru. "The prime minister's daughter, eh? Quite an honor to have you here, my dear."

"Getting beaten up on my behalf wasn't," Pru said.

But he shook his head before she could apologize. "All part of it, my dear. And it wasn't really so bad," he assured them, smiling as he headed toward the door. "You two saved me from worse."

But the way Pru saw it, Alvin and Elizabeth wouldn't have needed saving if she and Joshua had never come here in the first place.

Chapter 10

The man in the chair shrank against his ropes. Rather than appearing to be some deadly assassin, he looked terrified. His dark eyes were huge as they followed Joshua's every move and he seemed afraid of being beaten. There was a discoloration forming on his forehead where he had hit it against the floor when he'd gone down.

"I don't know who hired us," he cried for the third time. "I only know Malcolm and Conrad." He looked from the man to the woman he'd helped kidnap to the old woman he'd terrorized, clearly hoping for some pity. "Malcolm brought me along because I was handy with cars and he thought that maybe there'd be a need for that. I didn't even know who the hell we were supposed to be kidnapping until just now."

"And you're all right with that?" Pru demanded. "Just swooping down and kidnapping a defenseless woman for no reason?"

"You weren't defenseless. You bit me," the man, Ken, protested. "And there was a reason all right." It was obvious that this was not the brightest that the underworld had to offer. "Malcolm said that there'd be money, lots and lots of it. That your family would pay anything to get you back. And nobody was going to be hurt," he added nervously, as if that made everything all right. "He told me that, Malcolm did." He all but pouted as he said, "But then you shot Malcolm. And Conrad." His voice dropped as he looked at the form beneath the sheet.

Because it had upset the old woman to see the body, Pru had gotten a sheet and spread it over the dead man.

As if he didn't have a care in the world, Joshua cocked his weapon and aimed it at the third kidnapper. "And now I'm going to shoot you—unless you want to tell me the truth."

"I *am* telling you the truth," the man sobbed. "I don't know how else to say it. Conrad said he was taking orders from someone too high up for me to know about. That *he* was the only one who could talk to this guy. Conrad said the less I knew, the better." He tried to shrug and couldn't. The ropes were tight. "That was good enough for me." The kidnapper shifted his eyes toward Pru. "Please, it's the truth. So help me God, it's the truth."

"God can't help you once that one gets a notion in his head and starts going," Pru told him solemnly, nodding her head in Joshua's direction. She turned toward Elizabeth, taking the woman by the arm. "Maybe I'd better take you into the next room, Elizabeth. You won't want to see this."

"Take me," the man in the chair cried, trying desperately to get loose. "Take me to the next room. Don't leave me here with him. Please!"

"Maybe we shouldn't leave him in there," Elizabeth whispered to her the moment they were in the next room. The old woman looked concerned despite the fact that the man had tried to hurt her husband.

What a good soul this woman is, Pru thought. She shook her head. "Don't worry. Joshua's just trying to scare him," she told Elizabeth.

And then there was a scream. Elizabeth stiffened, her bright blue eyes widened. "Sounds like he's scared him plenty."

Any further speculation was curtailed as Joshua walked into the room, leaving his prisoner in the kitchen. "He doesn't know anything."

Pru took a breath as she glanced toward the other room. "Did you…kill him?"

Joshua shook his head and then laughed. "No, he fainted."

"Fainted? Then what was that scream we just heard?" she wanted to know.

"I cocked my weapon next to his head. Thought that if he had anything to tell me, that would do it. The fact that he fainted told me that he didn't and he was afraid he was going to die because of that." Frowning, he walked back into the other room and looked at the shape on the floor. "Looks like Malcolm here was the only man who knew anything." Squatting down, he removed the sheet from the body.

"Shouldn't touch anything," Elizabeth cautioned nervously, averting her eyes from the body. "It's a crime scene." She glanced at Pru. "I've seen all those American shows. They always say don't touch the body."

"That's because they're trying to find out who killed the victim and how," Joshua told the old woman, adding wryly, "I already know who killed him and how." Very carefully, he went through the man's pockets, looking for something that might connect him to whoever it was who had paid Malcolm, or whatever his real name was, to kidnap Pru. "What I need to know is who gave him his orders."

Malcolm's wallet was in his back pocket. Taking it out, Joshua found only a few bills, a receipt for a van rental and his driver's license.

"Malcolm Smythe," Joshua read, then snorted. "Not bloody likely." He committed the address to memory, just in case it might lead Lucia to something when he could finally get through to her. The rest of his search through the dead man's pockets only yielded a torn stub from a race track. "Obviously the man wasn't a winner," Joshua commented, rising. He made a quick decision. Better safe than sorry. "Prudence, we're going to have to get you out of here."

Elizabeth looked at him in surprise. He knew what the woman was thinking. That he'd promised to remain until Alvin returned.

"But my husband will be here any minute with the constable."

Joshua took the old woman's hand between both of his. "I'm sure you're more than capable of explaining to Constable Jeremy what happened here tonight."

In response, Elizabeth laughed almost shyly. "Yes, I suppose so."

"But why do we have to go?" Pru protested. "You got the men who were after me and I'm exhausted. Can't we just spend the night here?"

It was a lot more complicated than that. These sort of things always were.

"That bug they planted on you led the men who abducted you to this house. But they're not the only ones in on this," he reminded her. "That one——" he nodded at the man in the chair "——said that Malcolm was reporting to someone. I don't think we should just hang around and take a chance on the next team finding you here."

"The next team?" Pru echoed. This was a dream, a bad dream. A nightmare and any second now, she was going to wake up.

Elizabeth looked suddenly concerned as she took Pru's elbow. "Oh, my dear, he's right. You're not safe here. You have to go. Go." The old woman all but shooed them both toward the door.

Still Pru hesitated. She didn't like the idea of leaving an old woman with a potential killer, even if her husband and the constable were due shortly.

She looked at Elizabeth uncertainly. "You'll be all right?"

Elizabeth snorted and crossed her arms before her ample chest. "He's bound like a turkey and tied to a chair," she pointed out. "And besides, I have a skillet." Moving over to the cupboard, she took it out and wielded it in the air like a lethal weapon. "I'll be all right, dear," she promised. Elizabeth looked at Joshua. "You keep her safe."

"Yes, ma'am." Just as he was about to usher Pru out the front door, Joshua paused. "Is there an inn or a hotel somewhere in the vicinity?"

Elizabeth thought for a moment. "It's been a while since Alvin and I needed that sort of information. But I believe there's an inn about twenty kilometers due north of here. Robin's Nest, it's called." She looked uncertain about the matter as she added, "Some say it's haunted. Might even be torn down by now."

North instead of south. That placed them back around Haworth, he thought. But at least it was something. And people around here were not quick to tear anything down. "We'll give it a try."

Pru doubled back to hug the woman and thank her one last time. Rejoining Joshua, she waited until she was outside the house before she informed him, "I am *not* staying in a haunted inn."

His hand to her back, Joshua gently moved her along in case she decided to go back inside one last time. They had to get going. He had this feeling of urgency and although his feelings were not infallible, he knew better than to ignore them.

"At least the ghosts won't want to kidnap you."

Rather than take the newer vehicle, in case there was some way to track it, he decided it was best to continue with the truck. Joshua opened the passenger door for her and Pru got in.

"Very funny," she muttered.

Hobbling around the hood, he got in on the driver's side. She had a look on her face. By now, he recognized stubbornness on her when he saw it.

"You're serious, aren't you?" He started up the truck and then backed out of the driveway. "I thought you were an intelligent woman."

She didn't like his tone, or what he was implying. Pru crossed her arms and stared ahead, seeing nothing but darkness. "Intelligent enough to keep an open mind about things."

"Like spirits." He didn't bother trying to stifle a laugh.

Pru frowned. "There are more things in heaven and earth, Horatio, than are dreamt of in your philosophy," she said haughtily.

She was quoting Hamlet, he thought. Why was it that people always resorted to quoting famous lines when they couldn't make the point themselves? "People believed in ghosts in Hamlet's day," he reminded her.

"People believe in ghosts now," she countered. It wasn't that she actually believed in ghosts, but she didn't like feeling nervous in the dark and when things went bump in the night, that was enough to keep her up until first light. Something she really didn't need right now.

He glanced at her as he picked up a little speed. There was an entire stretch before them that wasn't buried in fog. "And why do *you* believe in ghosts?"

She blew out a breath, refusing to look at him even though she could feel his eyes on her. "Let's just say this isn't my first go-around at being kidnapped."

Pieces began to fall together. "The time you were ten."

So he knew about that. She'd forgotten that he had access to her file—whatever that really meant. She supposed that somewhere, within some government agency, there was an accounting of everything she had ever done since she'd been on solid food. The thought did not please her. She wasn't a fanatic about privacy, but it would have been nice to maintain a shred of it.

"The time I was ten," Pru agreed. "That time, they did want money." She looked out on the road grimly. "They locked me in the closet for three days. Three very long days and nights. In the dark."

Though he would never admit it to anyone, he'd gone through a phase of "monsters-in-the-dark" himself when he was eight. His father had ridiculed him for it and that was when he'd decided to tough it out and show his father what he was made of. He supposed, in a way, he'd been showing his father ever since.

"Well, since nothing came to whisk you away into the nether world during that time, that should have cured you."

"It didn't." It made her almost pathologically afraid of the dark for close to ten years. She still had relapses every so often. Those were the nights she slept with the light on. "I had a powerful imagination. Still do."

"Fair enough." Glancing at the odometer, he estimated they had another fifteen to eighteen kilometers to go. "Tell you what, when we get there, I'll stand guard while you sleep."

So now he didn't need sleep? "Are you going to tell me you're a robot?"

The question made him laugh. "I just don't need as much sleep as the average person. Besides, it's not all that many hours until dawn. Maybe by then, we'll be able to find a signal in this godforsaken place."

She'd detected a bit of an accent when he spoke, an accent that told her Joshua might have once been a native of Great Britain, but he didn't spend most of his time here now.

His dismissive tone offended her sense of patri-otism, though she didn't usually trot it out. "Don't you like England?"

"I don't like the countryside," he corrected. It was much too laid back for him. He found himself missing the noise, the pace that belonged to the city. "Give me urban life any time."

"Really?" She supposed that they were probably as opposite as possible. "I like the country. There's something uncomplicated and simple about it. Relaxing," she added, "away from places where buildings and people are all vying for space when there's a limited amount to be had."

It was an interesting philosophy for someone who lived in one of the most cosmopolitan cities in the world. "Then what are you doing in London?"

There were times when she asked herself just that. Especially during the wee hours of the morning, when everything about life felt unsettled, like shoes that didn't quite fit. And questions came to haunt her from every part of her mind.

"It was my father's idea, actually, although Uncle George advanced it. George Montgomery," she added when she saw him looking at her curiously. The man really wasn't her uncle, he was her father's best friend and a peacekeeper. He'd been the go-between when she and her father had had that rough patch that took her to third-world countries. "He wanted to keep the family 'close.'" Her smile was unreadable. "Good for his image and all that sort of thing."

Joshua studied her for a moment, then shook his head. He wasn't buying it. "I don't see you as someone who would obligingly go along with something like that for the sake of a political career."

"My *father's* political career," she pointed out.

"Even so."

He was either good at reading people, or at guessing, she thought.

"I wanted to go back to school, to get my doctorate." That had been her primary reason for returning to London after her stint in Africa. That and her new job at Feed the Children. "And I have to admit," she added grudgingly, "there are some interesting things about the city. The theater, for instance." She caught herself stifling a yawn. "God, I'm having trouble keeping my eyes open."

After what she'd been through today, he didn't understand why she hadn't collapsed the second she'd gotten into the truck. "Why don't you take a nap?" he suggested. "I'll wake you once we're at the inn."

The offer was tempting and for a moment, she considered it. "You're sure you know where you're going, Secret Agent Man?"

He had an inherent sense of direction that was rarely wrong. "Just get some sleep," he advised.

Pru stifled another yawn, then decided against taking a nap. The last time she'd closed her eyes, she'd opened them to find herself tied to a chair. She could hang on a little longer. "Thanks, but I think I should stay awake just in case you start to fall asleep at the wheel—even if you think you are a robot. No sense in taking any chances, right?"

He had enough adrenaline racing through his veins from the last incident to keep him going into the middle of next week. But he said nothing. Instead, he merely nodded. "Suit yourself."

She gave him a look that said she didn't need his permission for anything. "I usually do."

Pru had no idea exactly when she fell asleep. One moment, she was staring at the fog-enshrouded road, talking to Joshua about the Wakefields and how bad she felt about what might have happened to them because of her, the next she was opening her eyes and found that she was in his arms, being carried somewhere.

For just the smallest of fleeting seconds, still half asleep, Pru smiled, enjoying the sensation of being held by him. But the very next moment, she was fully conscious and awake. And on her guard.

"What are you doing?" she demanded, stiffening as she put her hands up against his chest, pushing him away from her. "I guess your leg is feeling better."

Afraid of dropping her, Joshua stopped walking. "Only way I knew how to get you out of the truck and into the inn," he told her tersely, knowing what was probably going through her mind. As if he needed to force himself on any woman. What kind of men did she know, anyway? "You sleep like a rock."

Maybe she believed him, maybe she didn't. But she knew that she didn't want to stay in his arms like this. It felt much too much like a tender trap and she wanted to keep her wits about her. Ever since she'd kissed him at the Wakefields', something odd was going on inside her and she refused to give it free rein.

"You can put me down now," she ordered.

"You don't have to ask me twice," he told her, setting her down so abruptly, she stumbled as she tried to get her footing.

She shot him an annoyed glance, then turned to look up at the building he'd brought her to.

With its peeling paint and sagging wood trim, Robin's Nest had definitely seen better decades, she thought. And the southern end looked as if it was in the middle of some sort of renovation that had been abruptly abandoned. From the look of it, business was not too good. The place was far from inviting.

Pru caught his arm before he took another step. "Maybe we should sleep in the truck."

"We're already here," he pointed out, although his tone seemed almost gentle to her. "Might as well see if there's anyone around." And then he said exactly the right thing to get her moving. "Not afraid, are you?"

She raised her chin and a look came into her eyes. The same kind of look he suspected her kidnappers had seen when she fought to get free. "No."

"Didn't think so," was all he said. Joshua walked into the building ahead of her.

The front desk was a few steps away from the entrance. There was a long, tall candle in the center of the desk, lighting a basket of snack bars, and it appeared to be the only source of illumination. Behind the desk was a clerk. They saw his bald head first. He was resting it on his crossed arms and appeared to be very soundly asleep.

Joshua shook him. When nothing happened, Joshua looked at Pru. "He sleeps like you." Pru made no reply. It took several attempts before the man woke up. When he did, he stared at them bleary-eyed.

And then it was as if a light bulb went off in his head. "Welcome to Robin's Nest," the man mumbled, saying the greeting as if he was trying to talk with a mouthful of marbles.

"We'd like a room," Joshua told him.

"With two beds," Pru interjected quickly. "No point in you sleeping on the floor," she said to Joshua.

The clerk shook his head. "Sorry, all our rooms come with one bed."

"That'll be fine," Joshua said before Pru could protest or walk out the door.

The man nodded. He turned around and took a key off the hook, holding it out to Joshua. But when the latter moved to take it, the clerk drew the key back just out of reach.

"That'll be sixty for the night. Don't figure you'll be staying on much longer than that."

"You figured right." Joshua took out his wallet and paid the man in cash rather than risk using any of the cards that he'd tucked away for emergencies. Money left no trail to follow. He took the key out of the desk clerk's hand.

"First door to your right at the head of the stairs," the clerk mumbled, settling back to continue his interrupted nap.

"He didn't look surprised that we didn't have any luggage," Pru observed as she followed Joshua up the stairs.

Joshua laughed shortly. "He probably deals with that a lot. He doesn't exactly seem like the type to have any regular interaction with a first-class clientele."

"This day just keeps getting better and better," Pru murmured under her breath as they came to the landing. There was debris in the hallway, a greasy bag from a fast-food restaurant left crumpled in the corner, cigarette butts here and there. The oppressive smell of sweat and cigarettes hung heavily in the air. It made her long for the rain.

"Doesn't he have anyone in to clean this place?" she demanded, annoyed, as she pushed aside the remnants of the cobweb she'd just walked into.

"I don't think the people who come here are really interested in the ambiance," Joshua commented.

He was right, she thought, looking around the room she had just walked into. The dark wallpaper made it seem that much smaller and drearier. There was a faint smell she couldn't place and had a feeling she was better off that way.

She'd slept on the ground in huts, she could do this. But not happily.

"Ghosts and prostitutes. This place has a lot going for it," she murmured, closing the door behind her.

But when Joshua brushed up against her to secure the lock, Pru forgot all about how objectionable the room was.

Chapter 11

"Sorry," he apologized, flipping the lock and securing the bolt above it before stepping back away from her. "Just want to make sure that no one's going to come in without effort."

She stared at the door. Short of succumbing to dynamite, it looked pretty impenetrable to her. "What do you mean, without effort?" She turned to look at him. It was too dark, she decided, crossing to the bureau and lighting one of the candles that appeared to be standard fare. Did these blackouts occur often? "You just locked the door. Shouldn't that keep people out?" she wanted to know.

"Should," he agreed, watching her. Noting the

way the light from the candle seemed to caress her face. "Run-of-the-mill people at any rate."

Her eyes met his. She was trying to brazen this out, but she was feeling a great deal less than brazen right now. For a number of reasons. "And you're worried about a superrace barging in, or people who are—?"

"Super determined," he said, completing her sentences.

She let out a long breath, running her hands along her arms even though it was far from cool in the room. Stuffy was more like it. "Really know how to make a girl feel at ease, don't you?"

Somehow, although he wasn't really sure just how, he was standing next to her again, despite the precautions he'd taken to create space between them. Space that seemed to have melted away of its own accord.

"Actually," he confessed, "I've never been accused of that."

The slight, sensual curve of his mouth told her exactly how he meant that. And she had to admit, being around him, when she wasn't completely focused on outrunning would-be kidnappers, did tend to raise her body temperature.

More than a little.

There was something sensually physical about this secret agent man. She'd seen better-looking men, but none who were more compellingly attractive in a magnetic sort of way.

"Maybe you should take classes, then," she suggested, trying to sound breezy and nonchalant. Trying to concentrate on anything other than the memory of the kiss they'd shared at the Wakefields' house and how it had brought her to the brink of a meltdown within thirty seconds. "Isn't that part of your job?" she pressed, desperate to keep talking, to keep her lips moving in the air rather than against him. "To make your subject feel at ease? Safe? Protected?"

Each word dripped from her lips in slow motion, like drops of water caught in a freeze-frame. Her eyes never left his. Damn, but her skin had to be about five degrees hotter than it had been a second ago.

"My job," he told her, standing so close now that a breeze would have to request space to pass between them, "*is* to protect you, to *make* you safe. And if that puts you at your ease, all well and good, if not, it's not important. Being safe is."

She'd felt safer standing on the edge of a cliff with a sheer fifty-foot drop inches away from her feet. "And am I, Secret Agent Man? Am I safe?" she breathed, looking up at him. "Here and now, am I safe?"

Joshua swallowed discreetly before answering. His throat had suddenly gone dry for no reason that he was comfortable exploring. But he held his ground. He never lied unless he absolutely had to.

"The truth?"

She slowly nodded, her eyes sealed to his. "Nothing but."

"No," he told her honestly.

But the danger he was thinking of wasn't coming from any outside source, wasn't due to some unseen, unknown high-ranking puppeteer located somewhere behind the scenes. The danger he was thinking of came from within. From him. And from the way he caught himself feeling as he took in a long breath only to have her scent fill up his head.

"Maybe I should be armed," she suggested, the words still coming in slow motion and in direct contrast to the way her heart insisted on beating this very moment.

"I'd say," he began, running his hands slowly along her bare arms, as if to somehow anchor himself to what was real, to his surroundings rather than what he was experiencing, "that you already are armed, Prudence." She really *was* beautiful, he caught himself thinking. "More than enough. Much more than enough," he whispered.

Cotton. The inside of her mouth had turned to pure cotton. "Then I should be safe, shouldn't I?"

"Should be," he agreed softly.

How was it that her heart hadn't broken through her chest yet? And why was it beating so hard? She wasn't some blushing vestal virgin who'd never been alone with a man. There'd been lovers. Not a squadron, but enough.

And for the life of her, she couldn't remember the name, or the face, of a single one of them.

"But I'm not," she concluded out loud in a husky whisper.

"No."

For one sweet, sultry moment, she thought Joshua was going to kiss her. He was still holding her arms and he'd bent his head, giving every indication that full body contact was imminent.

And then he took a long breath and rather than bring his mouth down to hers, he used his hands to move her back, away from him. If lightning had struck her, she couldn't have been more surprised. Or disappointed.

"I'll take the floor and first watch," he told her, dropping his hands.

Dazed, Pru felt as if she was coming out of a wild tailspin, disoriented and unable to tell which was the ground and which was the sky.

Was the bastard toying with her? Seeing how far he could push this before she came unglued and jumped his bones?

Embarrassed, humiliated, Pru doubled up her fist and punched his arm as hard as she could. Which was considerable.

Joshua saw it coming. He tensed his arm a split second before contact was made and thus her fist pretty much met rock. At least it certainly felt like it. It took everything she had not to grab her knuckles and give voice to the pain that was slicing through her.

"All right," he said evenly, as if he knew why she'd just unleashed a right cross at him, "you can have first watch."

"That wasn't about 'first watch' or the damn bed," she snapped. Turning her back, she moved away from him and toward the window.

Joshua was less than a step behind her, drawing the curtains so that her image remained locked within the room instead of being broadcast outside. He was taking absolutely no chances. He wasn't about to be caught napping again.

"Then what is it about?" he wanted to know, facing her.

Instead of answering him, she asked a question of her own. "How have you managed to remain alive all this time, Secret Agent Man? Why hasn't some woman skewered you yet?"

"Why?" Unable to help himself, Joshua found the distance between them melting again. Found himself gently pushing back the hair from her face and looking into eyes the color of shamrocks. Mesmerized. "Is that what you want to do?"

She raised her chin, a bantam weight ready to go the distance. "It's on the list."

His fingers curled into her hair, lightly grazing the outline of her ear. Desire stirred. "What else is on that list?"

"Wouldn't you like to know?"

Her heart was hammering in her throat. She desperately wanted to hit him again. And keep hitting him so that she didn't make a fatal mistake and fling herself into his arms.

Or worse, kiss him.

The way she wanted to with all her soul.

"Yes," he told her quietly, so quietly that the breath that accompanied the words lightly moved along her skin, "I would."

The next moment, the decision to kiss or not to kiss was taken out of her hands.

If errors were going to be made, they would be his to initiate, Joshua thought. He brought his mouth down to hers and kissed her. Kissed her hard, with all the barely reined-in feelings that were threatening to erupt within him.

Rather than bringing her to her senses and making her back away, fleeing for her life, his kiss had the opposite effect. It made all sorts of sensations explode within her. Made her recall that it had been a very long time since she'd felt passion even close to this level.

Maybe this was malaria, she thought, desperate for an explanation. Or some rare, tropical disease, making her hallucinate. Making her feel things that she wasn't really feeling. She had no idea, no explanation for what was happening to her. All she knew was that she didn't want this to stop at any threshold. Not with a kiss, not with an embrace.

Not for a very long time.

Damn, she was trembling, Joshua realized. What's more, almost perversely, her reaction was turning him on in a way he couldn't even begin to describe or to understand. All he knew was that he wanted her, wanted her with a vast, deep, belly-gnawing hunger that left him reeling and unable to do anything but continue what he was doing.

He was going straight to hell after this.

But somehow, the journey—and the eternal stay—would be worth it. To his way of thinking, he was trading eternity for something very precious, something he'd never experienced before. A passion so great, it created a pocket of fear within him.

Because it was in control of him, he was not in control of it and that, he thought, any way you looked at it, was a very bad thing.

But he'd think about that later, later when the wee hours of the morning crept over him on tiny feet, scratching his soul and making him repent for every wrong he'd ever done. This, he knew, would be at the head of the list.

Knowing it didn't stop him.

He moved his hands along Pru's taut, firm body as if to reassure himself that she was real, that this hallucination that had spun out of the depths of his wanting was real for the moment.

Her skin was like cream, her flesh as hot as his.

He couldn't remember every detail, although he wanted to. She was dressed, then she wasn't. Within a heartbeat, her firm, slim body was against his, setting a match to his soul.

She was tugging urgently at his clothing as he pushed her back against the bed, moving with her as she fell against the covers. He shrugged off the borrowed shirt, shucked the borrowed pants. His naked body pressed against hers as an urgency filled his veins, begging for quick, satisfying relief.

But that would be satisfying himself on the basest of levels and it had never been about that for him. That would have made him like his father and Joshua would have had himself castrated before he ever allowed that to happen.

So rather than thrust himself into her, he held back and made love to her with his hands, with his mouth, with his very breath as it moved along her skin. Beginning with her toes and working his way up slowly.

She twisted and turned beneath him, sounds escaping her lips that told him it was not anguish that governed her but ecstasy.

It made holding back possible.

With skillful touches, he discovered places that made her whimper. Places that made her bite down on her lower lip to keep from crying out. Places that brought her from one climax to the next. He almost experienced one of his own, just stroking her. Holding himself in check was taking more and more effort.

But her passivity lasted only as long as her stunned awe did. And then, without warning, Pru moved and took up the dominant role.

She was making his body sing. She was pressing warm, openmouthed kisses along his flesh, teasing him with her tongue, hardening him so that it took almost superhuman strength to keep from taking possession of her and sealing himself within her.

She made his head spin, his blood run hot as it surged within his veins.

And then, suddenly, his strength threatened to desert him.

A man could only hold out for so long.

With a guttural cry that bordered on the primal, Joshua switched positions, rolling her back flat against the bed. Parting her legs with his knee, he lowered himself onto her and sheathed himself within her, doing his best not to let the almost overwhelming urgency throbbing within him spill out. He wasn't going to let her think of him as some rutting animal.

The moment he was within her, it was a struggle not to take her within a heartbeat. With the last thread of control, Joshua orchestrated his movements. The tempo grew fast quickly. He began to move hard and with an urgency that took both their breaths away.

Pru lifted her hips, trying to sustain the rhythm he created, trying to let it continue rather than sweep them away. But each pass brought them closer to the top of the summit.

And then it was reached.

The next second they fell over the side, clinging to one another, wrapped in an exhilarating moment that made their blood pound as one.

When it was over, when the sensation had ebbed back like the retreating tide, Joshua all but collapsed against her, exhausted beyond words.

Were he a normal man, with a normal life, he would have gladly just fallen asleep that way, sheathed in her as well as ecstasy. But he wasn't a normal man with a normal life and indulging himself would have left them both vulnerable. Especially her.

And whether the prime minister's daughter realized it or not, Joshua thought, for the duration, his life was pledged to protect hers.

It took him a moment to catch his breath as he rolled off Pru and gathered her to him. It bothered him that he felt as if he barely had enough strength for that. Closing his eyes, he prayed that no one would choose this moment to attack.

Definitely going to hell for this, he told himself.

"So," he finally managed to say, measuring his words in order not to sound breathless, "what else did you say was on that list?"

She laughed then, her breasts rising and falling, brushing against his arm and creating fresh tidal waves within the pit of his stomach. Damned if he didn't want her all over again.

Probably hadn't the strength to act on that desire, he thought, but it didn't stop desire from taking root and infiltrating his mind, seductively whispering along his all but spent body.

"I think, Secret Agent Man, that we just managed to burn the whole list." She took a long, deep breath, wondering just when her heart was going to stop racing and return to normal. Right now, the answer felt like never. She turned her body toward his, for the moment blissfully unself-conscious in her nudity. "So, is this how you 'take care of' all your assignments?"

Joshua raised himself up on his elbow, looking down at her face. He looked very serious, she thought.

"No," he told her without even a hint of a smile. "This is a first."

For a second, she thought he was referring to making love. Just how simple did he think she was?

Pru studied him for a moment. "And you were a virgin before this," she teased. "What about that teacher you said you seduced when you were, what? Fifteen?" she reminded him.

"She was never my assignment," he pointed out, then added, "I've never mixed business with pleasure before, Pru."

She noticed he'd used her nickname instead of the given one she hated. Was that a slip, or on purpose? Because he knew she preferred it, or to get her off her guard? Her head ached.

"Never?" she wanted to know.

Joshua moved his head from side to side slowly. "Never."

"And if I were to believe you—" her tone indicated to him that for at least now, she didn't "—what makes me so special that you broke your 'never' rule?"

This time he did smile, just a little, as he toyed with the ends of her hair. "If you have to ask, then maybe you're not the woman I took you for."

Something bubbled up within her, a giddiness that seemed to materialize out of nowhere. She felt like laughing and she had no idea why. She knew better than to believe the word of a man who was just passing through her life.

And yet…

And yet there was something inside her that really wanted to believe. In love, in knights in shining armor. In him.

"And just what kind of woman did you take me for, Secret Agent Man?"

Joshua paused for a moment, as if he was giving her question serious consideration. "Feisty, intelligent, feisty, witty—did I say feisty?"

Her mouth curved invitingly. She shifted her body a little closer to his. Even as she did so, she could feel it humming. Anticipating. "You did."

He inclined his head, pressing a kiss to her shoulder. "Bears repeating."

His breath tickled her. She didn't bother pretending that she wasn't reacting. "Yes," she agreed, smiling as she threaded her arms around his neck. "It does."

It didn't take a rocket scientist to understand her meaning.

Cassandra paced around the spacious suite that had once belonged to her father and now served as her bedroom. It was three in the morning.

She didn't sleep much anymore.

The last few months, sleep had begun to visit her

less and less. And when it came, it rarely remained for very long, slipping away like a guest afraid of overstaying his welcome.

It was because her mind never stopped working. She couldn't allow it to. She had not gotten where she was by letting nature take its course, or by letting "the men" handle things. She was at the head of this vast, powerful organization not because she was her father's daughter but in spite of it.

Because Maximilian had wanted to pass this to a male heir. After Apollo had died, he'd tried to groom others for the position. Others whom she had secretly taken care of, either on her own, or by making use of the men who succumbed to her. Until finally, she'd put an end to it, an end to her father's search.

An end to her father.

It was necessary. He'd been her weakness. Because she loved him when he didn't love her.

Men. They were useless. All useless. Her father, her brother, the men who now bore alliance to her, they were all mere pawns for her to use in her plan to become an ultimate force to be reckoned with.

Even Troy, the child she'd taken to her breast, the son she had christened with her name, even he was guilty of the same sins as the others of his gender.

But for him, she had hope. Because she had schooled him to follow her path, to think her thoughts. To become the shadow of her ambition.

And when the time came, she would use him.

Use him to strike at the man she'd once thought different from all the others.

The man she was now bent on making repentant with every breath he took. Until there were no more breaths to take.

She raised the receiver to her ear, pressing a single button. The other end was picked up before the first ring was completed.

As it should be.

"Well?" she demanded sharply.

A voice on the other end said, "Malcolm is dead, as is Conrad. Ken was arrested."

"Kill him." Her voice was flat as she struggled to contain her rage. She would *not* be bested. "And send in the second team." Cassandra let the receiver drop back into the cradle and rose, crossing to the window.

She drew aside the drapes and stared into the moonlight, wishing she could sleep.

Chapter 12

The room was stuffy. He didn't dare open the windows. That would be courting disaster. Long ago, he'd learned there was no such thing as too safe.

And at the heart of the reckless life he led, he always played it safe.

That, he was beginning to think, sitting on the side of the bed and looking at the woman he'd made love with for a good part of the night, included the women he'd had. Wild, sensual, sexual, they were still all safe. Safe because he wouldn't have wound up at the end of the month with any of them.

But this one…

This one had to be protected, he reminded himself tersely. Everything else was just secondary. Or inconsequential.

Joshua glanced at his watch. They'd already been here too long. Too long in one place. He didn't like to tempt fate.

Because he knew she was exhausted, he'd let her sleep as long as he could and even now, he was loath to wake her. But he knew he had to.

Against his practical nature, Joshua paused a moment longer, just watching her sleep. The spitfire looked a great deal more peaceful this way than she had since he'd met her.

It was hard for him to believe that was less than twenty-four hours ago. It felt more like a lifetime. They'd fought, run for their lives and made love in less time than it took to marinate a fine steak. They'd packed the last half of the day to the bursting point. It was going to be a long time before he forgot any of it.

Especially the lovemaking.

They'd made love one more time before finally falling asleep. At least, she'd fallen asleep. He had learned the art of sleeping with one eye open when he joined the Lazlo Group. He couldn't remember when he'd actually gotten a full night's rest, even on holiday.

But she had certainly done her best to iron out all the kinks in his body, Joshua thought with a smile. Too bad there was no time for an encore.

Although, now that he thought of it, he had a feeling that in the light of day, she would probably push him away. Nothing about Prudence Hill, he was learning, was simple or easy.

But then, that was what made her interesting. And him interested.

Placing a hand on her shoulder, he gently shook Pru. "Rise and shine, princess."

In response, Pru, still firmly entrenched in a dreamless sleep, merely swatted his hand away and rolled over on her side.

God, but she looked delicious, he thought, then roused himself. There was no time to get distracted, or get lost in the rise and fall of the curves of her anatomy. It was almost six. The sun had been up for a while now. And they had to get going.

"Sorry, Prudence." He shook her shoulder again, more forcefully this time. "We need to get going. If nothing else, we've got a limited amount of time to get to your father and I don't want to cut it too close or get too cocky about making it." And then he smiled. "Even though after last night, I feel that wouldn't exactly be that much of a stretch."

Last night.

Pru's eyes flew open. The next second, as her mind focused, she bolted upright. And realized, as she sucked in air, that she was still very nude and right now, the object of Joshua's very intent stare.

Indignant, embarrassed, Pru grabbed the edges of the comforter on either side and yanked it close to her, even as she felt her skin shrinking back from the fabric. Being wrapped in a less-than-clean comforter was still better than being exposed to Joshua's unrelenting scrutiny. Didn't he have any decency?

"What do you think you're doing?" she demanded angrily.

A gentleman would have looked away. But a gentleman wouldn't have made love with her like that last night. And he wasn't a hypocrite unless he had to be. "Looking at one of the very best bodies I've had the privilege in my lifetime to see." And then he raised his eyes to her face. "However, we do need to be on our way," he urged. "Bad guys," he reminded her in case she'd forgotten.

Pru took him literally and immediately scanned the area. "Where?"

"That's just it, we don't know." He moved about the room, pacing. Impatient to be gone. "So we need to hit the road and keep things in our favor." He stopped at the foot of the bed.

"Turn around," she ordered.

This time, he stared more intently. What was this nonsense? "Excuse me?"

Pru twirled her index finger downward in the air, indicating motion. "Turn around. If you want me to get dressed, you have to turn around."

"I'm the one who *un*dressed you, remember?" Finding the whole thing oddly humorous, Joshua did as she asked and turned his back to her. "There's no reason to suddenly turn shy on me, Pru. I'm the same guy whose clothes you almost ripped off last night."

"I wasn't ripping," she protested. "My nails got caught in the material." It was a lame excuse, but it was all she had.

"If you say so," he answered in a singsong tone that told her the exact opposite. "Although I have to admit this sudden modesty is rather sweet in an old-fashioned sort of way."

Pru bit back a few choice words. He was patronizing her, she thought angrily. She hated being patronized.

"It didn't mean anything you know," Pru told him heatedly as she hurried into her clothes. "Last night," she clarified in case she'd lost him. "It didn't mean anything. I wasn't myself."

He laughed shortly, shaking his head. Picking up the holster, he rested his foot on the bed and moved his pant leg up, exposing his calf. "Whoever you sent in your place was one hell of an athletic wonder," he commented, strapping his weapon to his calf before lowering the pant leg back into place. It was hidden to all but the well-practiced eye.

"I do that sort of thing all the time." She did her best to sound casual, dismissive. Anything but the way she felt. Like a tender-footed cat on a tin roof sizzling beneath the July sun. "There's nothing to single you out."

He accepted that the way he did everything else. With a grain of salt. She was too adamant when she said it. The line about Lady Macbeth protesting too much ran through his head, but he refrained from saying it out loud. He had no desire to agitate her. Yet.

"Nice to know I blend in so well with the rest of the male population," he replied crisply. It was time to cut through the bull. He knew why she was saying what she was. It was a trust issue. "Look, Pru. I'm not about to sell the story about last night to the nearest tabloid. You can stop worrying."

Pru took instant umbrage. "I'm not worrying," she snapped. "I'm—" And then, just like that, she ran out of steam. Slanting a look in his direction, Pru asked, "You're not?"

"No." Not above needling her just a little, he added, "It would ruin my cover."

She couldn't explain why, since she'd expected nothing more from him, there was this sinking feeling in her stomach when Joshua said that. "Is that the only reason?"

Really in a hurry now, he still spared her one intense look. "What do you think?"

Warmth crept over her. The kind of warmth that led to acts that were less than prudent. The irony almost made her smile. She straightened her shoulders. "I think we'd better do as you said and get out of here."

"That's my girl—in only the most general sense of the word," he quickly qualified when she looked at him sharply.

The look didn't fade. Now what the hell was going on? he wondered, hustling her out the door.

The same clerk from last night was at the desk, in the exact position they'd originally found him. With his head cradled against the registry where they had signed in last night under false names.

Except that this time, the position had become permanent.

The air caught in Pru's lungs. She opened her mouth. Whether to scream, protest or make a vehement disclaimer she wasn't sure but she never got a chance to express any of it. Joshua's hand clamped over her mouth.

Shock telegraphed through her as she continued to stare at the clerk. There was blood, fresh blood. Pooling just beneath the man's head, seeping onto the pages of the guest registry.

Slowly removing his hand from her mouth, Joshua indicated the door they'd just walked through with a sharp nod of his head. He didn't have to do it twice. She was ready to flee the minuscule lobby in a heartbeat.

In her wake, Joshua quickly looked behind the front desk, looking for the clerk's killer. There was no one in the area but the three of them. The killer was nowhere in sight.

And then he was.

He heard Pru stifle a strangled cry of surprise. Instincts took over immediately.

The doorway was blocked by a wiry, thin man not much taller than she was. He had the coldest eyes she'd ever seen.

"You've given us a lot of trouble, Miss Hill."

"Pru, drop!"

Instantly, she went limp, falling flat on the floor just as the man was about to reach for her. A shot whizzed above her head. She could almost feel its vibration as she heard metal meet bone.

The next second, she was being yanked to her feet and propelled forward, forced to step over the body of the man who was no longer a threat to her.

But still the nightmare was continuing.

Her eyes scanned the area, looking for others. For more. "Who *are* these people?" she demanded breathlessly, bursting out the front door.

"The best damn trackers I've ever run into," was all Joshua said. Rather than the vehicle he'd left parked in the lot last night, he hurried her into the only other car in sight, a sleek, black sedan.

The smell of new leather faintly registered as she fumbled with the seat belt. The killer's car? "What about the truck?" she wanted to know.

"Low on petrol," Joshua retorted, annoyed that even at a time like this, she was constantly challenging him, demanding explanation. The car sputtered to life. He dropped the two wires he'd brought together and grabbed hold of the wheel.

As he drove away, flooring the accelerator, he

looked in the rearview mirror. Another man was running out of the inn, brandishing a gun.

"Duck!" Joshua ordered.

"Why?" she cried. "There's no one up ahead."

Rather than argue with her, Joshua covered her head with his hand and physically pushed Pru down far into her seat.

Just as something whizzed through the vehicle on her side.

"There's more," she lamented in disbelief, staying down.

"There's more," he confirmed grimly.

He drove like a man possessed.

Pru looked over her shoulder at the black sedan that she and Joshua had just spent the last ten minutes covering up with broken branches and loose shrubbery so that it wasn't visible from the road. They were now quickly putting distance between themselves and the vehicle. She'd followed orders, but not willingly. It made no sense to her.

"Why are we abandoning the car?" she asked for the third time, her tone indicating that she wasn't going to be satisfied with just going along with this. "Can't we just drive it to London?" That would have made more sense to her.

"Because they'll be looking for it," he told her. Not to mention that the car might have a built-in tracking device or be rigged to self-destruct after a given point if a code wasn't properly input on it.

He'd taken it because he knew it was faster, because it had temporarily left Pru's would-be abductors without their own transportation and because it had gas. But keeping the car was pushing their luck.

She sighed, not at all happy with this change in venue. "So we're walking?"

He looked at her, an amused smile curving the corners of his mouth. "I'd never make the prime minister's daughter walk."

What was that supposed to mean? Was he lapsing into some kind of riddle? "We're walking now." She gestured at the dirt path they were on.

"To London," he qualified, feeling remarkably even-tempered, given the circumstances. "I'd never make the prime minister's daughter walk all the way to London."

"So where *are* we going in the middle of nowhere?" she wanted to know. "With your bum leg," Pru tagged on, looking down at the leg she'd taken a bullet out of not that many hours ago.

"My leg is not bum," he informed her calmly. "It's healing." And then he heard a rumbling noise in the distance. "At least, I hope it is," Joshua murmured under his breath.

Her eyes widened. The noise continued, coming closer. "More thunder?" She didn't think she could bear the idea of more rain.

"No, a train," he corrected, picking up pace. "Our train."

She hurried to catch up to him. It didn't take

much. And, despite everything, it felt good to run. "What do you mean, our train?"

He focused on the road. His thigh suddenly felt as if it had burst into flames, but he gave no indication, refused to allow himself the distraction. "We're taking the train to London."

Keeping pace, she looked around. There were only trees, although she could make out some tracks up ahead. Where were they boarding the train? "There's a train station out here in the middle of nowhere?"

He could feel perspiration forming at his temples, down his spine. "No."

She was in no frame of mind for another one of his puzzles. "Then how are we supposed to get on the train?" she demanded.

He continued focusing on reaching where they needed to be in order to get on, shutting his mind to the pain that was shooting up and down his leg, begging him to stop. "It's a freight train."

For a man with a bad leg, he ran like a fox with a pack of hounds at his heels, she thought in amazement. She was beginning to breathe harder. "That still doesn't answer my—" And then it hit her. "Oh, no. No. You can't mean—" Her voice trailed off. Joshua made no attempt to refute anything, and she was forced to put her thoughts into words. "We're not going to 'hop a freight.'" Was that the proper term for it? "Are we?"

He clenched his hands into fists and pumped his

arms, willing himself not to stumble. "That, Prudence Hill, is exactly what we're going to do."

Was he out of his mind? "Look, you might leap tall buildings in a single bound, but as for me, I run at a normal speed." There was no way she could catch up to a train.

"You're being modest." He took a deep breath, letting it out again as evenly as he could. "I saw the clip of you jogging. You're very fast."

Did he think he was going to flatter her into running faster? She couldn't, not even if she wanted to show him up. "Not as fast as a train."

He realized that he'd forgotten to give her a crucial piece of information. "The train slows down just up ahead."

For someone who avoided the countryside, he seemed to know an awful lot about the area. The operative word here was *seemed* and she wasn't totally convinced that he knew what he was talking about. "And you know this how?"

He'd studied the terrain and key points, such as train lines, something he always did when he was going into a place. He made it a point never to go in without an exit plan. But he needed to save his breath, so he merely said, "There's a sharp curve. Trust me."

Right, easy for him to say. But then, she'd driven down an incline with him, had him shoot men who were trying to kill her and made love with him in a crumbling inn. She supposed if that didn't inspire trust, nothing would.

"Lead on," she told him.

They cut across a field and were just at the curve when the freight appeared in the distance, barreling down. "Run faster," he ordered, barely getting the words out.

She did, but at the same time, she thought it was an exercise in futility. "We're never going to get on that train."

"Where's your optimism?" Flagging, he fell back behind her. "Keep running," he ordered. "Don't look back. Get on the first car with open doors or a flatbed."

In the end, he was right, the train did almost come to a stop because the curve was difficult to negotiate at top speed. Three cars went by before a flatbed car appeared. With a burst of energy, Joshua managed to get on just as the train reached its lowest speed.

"C'mon!" he cried, extending his hand to her. "You can do it. Where's all that feministic pride?" he goaded her.

He knew what to say, what buttons to press. Cursing him, she ran faster, grabbed hold and was pulled aboard. She tumbled onto the wooden slats and lay there, gasping for air.

Continuing to curse him in her mind because she had no energy to push the words out.

Just like in the old movies, she thought, vowing never to watch one again.

Pru continued to lie there, the rumbling of the train vibrating through her entire body. After a few moments, she realized that Joshua was on his feet. Now what? Opening her eyes, she saw that he was standing over her.

"C'mon."

She made no effort to sit up. "If you want me to run across the roofs, forget it."

He laughed and took her hand. "No roofs, I promise. Just across a coupling."

"Why?" she demanded. Wasn't that dangerous? If the train lunged, they'd wind up on the tracks. He might have a death wish, but she didn't.

He continued to hold his hand out to her. "Because we need to have walls and doors around us. I don't want to stay out in the open like this."

He was right, damn him. Grudgingly, she sat up and gave him her hand. He pulled her to her feet. "You're enjoying this, aren't you?"

"Sunny day, beautiful woman, ride in the country, what's not to enjoy?" he quipped.

"You are certifiable, you realize that."

He saw no point in arguing. Anyone who faced death on a regular basis operated by a different set of rules. "Most likely."

Very carefully, he picked his way across the coupling between the two cars and opened the door leading into the next, closed car. From the looks of it, it was hauling tractor parts. There was little room for maneuvering. Joshua found a space where they could sit.

Pru all but collapsed onto the floor. Sitting, she

pulled up her knees and rested her head against them. She wondered if her pulse would ever get back to normal.

"What are you afraid of?"

The question broke the rhythmic rattle of the train as it made its way from the country to the city. She'd almost dozed off, she realized.

Now she raised her head and looked at him. It was an odd question, but then, everything since she'd met him had been odd. "Aside from ghosts and kidnappers popping up between the rails?"

One side of his mouth rose in a half smile. "Aside from that."

She took a deep breath and then tossed her head. "Nothing."

He wasn't buying it. "Don't give me that. Back at the inn, you had this look in your eyes when I said 'that's my girl,' like we were suddenly on opposite sides of the fence and you were about to pick up your broadsword."

She looked away from him, annoyed. So now he was going to add analyst to his list of accomplishments? "I haven't got the faintest idea what you're talking about, Secret Agent Man."

"Yes, you do." His voice was almost gentle. It put her on her guard. "Somebody hurt you, Pru?"

Where did he get off, asking her something like that? It was far more personal than making love. He was asking to look into her soul. "I'd have to care for someone to hurt me."

He'd struck a nerve, he thought. "Yes," he agreed, "you would. Did he?"

She forgot to be tired. Only angry. "There is no 'he,' Secret Agent Man. There's never been a 'he.'"

Instead of arguing, the way she expected him to, he nodded. "So your dossier indicated, I thought that maybe you were just exceptional at hiding the identity of a significant other. 'She' then, although I have to say that after last night, if there was a 'she,' it's a horrible waste of talent."

The man just didn't stop, did he? Just because he'd saved her life once—twice, she amended—didn't give him the right to pry like this. "No, no 'she,' no 'he.'" Maybe this would shut him up. "I know better than to get close to people."

For a second, it sounded as if she'd taken a page out of his book. He knew why he was the way he was, but that didn't answer his questions about her.

"Oh? Why?"

She blew out a breath, clearly annoyed. The answer she gave came from between clenched teeth. "Because when you get close to people, you get used to seeing them there. Expect to see them there. And when they're suddenly not there, it hurts." She waved her hand dismissively. "I don't have time to be hurt."

"But you were." The look in her eyes confirmed it. "Your mother? Father?"

"No."

She'd said that too fiercely. "You're lying, Prudence." He took a stab at it. "Your mother died and that made you feel abandoned. But your father needed support, so you quickly retooled yourself to accommodate him. If you were busy, you couldn't think. Besides, you were needed." He watched her eyes as he spoke. "You became the perfect little hostess. Your father's right hand even though you hated all that travel, all that uprooting. And then suddenly, he got married. There was someone else to take over all the public duties, all the private talks. You were out in the cold—"

Damn him, for two cents, she'd push him off the train. "I get along perfectly well with my step-mother," she informed him angrily.

"I never said you didn't." She was, after all, despite the tabloid stories, a fair person. She didn't hate merely to hate. "But it wasn't the same, was it? The dynamics of your family changed and you were odd girl out."

She rose to her feet, wanting to be anywhere but near him. There was no place to go, no place to move. "You make me sound pathetic."

He rose to stand beside her. "You're not pathetic, Prudence. You're human. Anyone would feel the sting. Is that when you started to act out? Right after your father got married, you started bashing photographers over the head."

Damn, was she ever going to outlive that story? "Photographer," she corrected heatedly. "It was only one photographer and he wouldn't take his camera out of my face. Worse, he was trying to get photographs of my stepmother and her baby."

He'd read the story. Like all yellow journalism, there'd been a thread of truth in it. "Your half brother."

She hated that term. "Brett," Pru told him. "And he's not half of anything. I don't do things by halves, Lazlo. He's my brother. And Alexis is my sister and Gerald's my brother," she added, referring to her stepmother's children.

His eyes didn't leave hers. "And they're all part of your father's new family."

What did he want from her? "Look, what is your point? Why are you harping on this? You're worse than a tabloid photographer," she told him, wishing there was somewhere to go in this claustrophobic freight car, somewhere where she didn't have to look at him.

Part of him wondered why he was bothering. The other part knew, which worried him somewhat. Caring about someone seriously blunted his edge.

"My point is that it's all right to let people in, Pru. It's all right to feel."

She laughed shortly. There was no humor in her eyes. "Well, if you say so, Secret Agent Man, I guess it must be true."

He smiled, touching her cheek. Watching something come into her eyes. Feeling it stir him. "Now you're getting the hang of it."

Chapter 13

Mayday.

The single word telegraphed itself through Pru's brain, putting every single fiber of her being on high alert. She felt as if the swaying floor beneath her feet was about to open up, allowing her to drop down onto the tracks to be run over.

Nothing felt solid.

Except for the feel of his arms as they wound around her.

Time stood still. Then evaporated completely as he lowered his mouth to hers.

He was kissing her. Kissing her and making her forget every single word she'd just uttered in protest of attachments, taking great pains to point out the reason a rational person shouldn't feel anything for anyone. She could no longer hide behind that. Because, damn it, she *was* feeling, feeling things for him even when she didn't want to.

Her body leaned into his, whether through centrifugal force or because she was seeking the comfort that came from complete contact, she didn't know. All she knew was that one moment, there was a micron of space between them, the next they were closer than two pages in a book stashed beneath an anvil.

Heat, tension and yearning all built up to a dangerous level, threatening to burn her, to consume her.

And then, just as unexpectedly as he'd kissed her, he drew back. Her heart was hammering in her throat, making swallowing a challenging feat.

Joshua leaned his forehead against the top of her head. His voice was incredibly seductive when he asked, "Hungry?"

Yes, God help her, she was. Hungry with such intensity that she hardly recognized herself. Hungry to make love with him again despite all her rhetoric this morning about how the lovemaking they'd shared the night before hadn't meant anything.

It had.

It did.

And she wanted him again. So badly that her body ached and felt as if it was on the verge of disintegrating without him. Still, a shred of common sense managed to prevail.

"We can't do it here," she protested, dropping her arms and stepping back.

Distance, she needed distance. Distance from him, from the tempting scent of his breath, the arousing scent of his body. But there was no distance to be had, unless she felt like climbing up into the cab of the crane that was being transported in this car.

He looked at her curiously, clearly puzzled. Good, she thought, his turn for a change. "Why not?"

How could he ask that? Didn't surrounding conditions factor into this at all for him? Was he raised in a barn? "Because it's crammed and dirty. We'd have to do it standing up."

He still looked as if he didn't follow her. "What's wrong with that?"

"Nothing," she heard herself saying. If he couldn't figure it out, she wasn't about to try to explain it to him. "Not a damn thing." But as she began to put her arms around his neck again, Joshua surprised her by stepping back and producing a granola bar out of his back pocket. She stared at it. "What's this?"

"Breakfast." Neither one of them had time to get anything to eat before they fled the inn. "I grabbed it from the basket when we checked in at Robin's Nest," he added when she looked at him in confusion.

"Oh." She hadn't seen the food. Not when they went in and certainly not when they left. She had

been moving too fast to be on the lookout for anything other than would-be abductors materializing
out of thin air like the skeleton army in the Greek
myth, Jason and the Golden Fleece.

"You said you were hungry." He looked at her as
if he still didn't understand what she was thinking.

"I am." To prove it, she quickly took the granola
bar from him and ripped off the wrapper. "I just
thought you meant—never mind."

It was better that he didn't know what she meant,
she thought. He'd probably think she was over-
sexed—or had succumbed to his fatal charm.

Well, haven't you? a little voice whispered in her
head. She did her best to ignore it, giving her full attention to the swiftly disappearing honey, nut and
caramel bar.

And then it obviously dawned on him. He grinned
broadly, tickled. "You thought I was talking about
another kind of hunger."

"No," she retorted sharply, her mouth still filled
with peanuts.

He gave her a look that said he saw right through
her. "Prudence, we've been through too much for
you to lie to me now."

He'd probably lie to her in a heartbeat, she
thought. And never blink an eye. "All right. Here's
a truth for you: I hate being called Prudence."

He let the other matter drop. For now. "What shall
I call you?" he wanted to know. It was, after all, her
name. "Sam?"

"Whatever." She focused her attention on the granola bar. It was easier than trying to talk her way out of an embarrassing mistake. She had a hunch that the more she talked, the worse it would get. It was only after she'd devoured almost the entire bar that she realized Joshua wasn't eating anything. "Where's your granola bar?"

The shrug was indifferent. He was accustomed to going long periods without food. Part of the training. "I was only able to get one."

"Why didn't you say anything?" Damn, she felt like a glutton, even though the bar had been small. "I would have broken it in half. Here." She offered him the smattering of nuts and the smallest of crumbs that were still in her hand.

He laughed, pushing her hand back. "That's okay, you can finish it. I'm not hungry."

The hell he wasn't. "The can of oil fill you up, Tin Man?"

"Just about," he deadpanned back. He smiled as she dusted one hand against the other, getting rid of the last of the crumbs.

She had a feeling that he was looking right through her. And seeing things she didn't want him to see. "What?"

"Now," he said quietly, running his knuckles lightly along her cheek, "about that other hunger."

Heat instantly rose up through her body. What *was* it about this man that made her feel like an awkward, simpering adolescent? She absolutely *hated* not feeling in control of things and ever since Joshua had come into her life, everything had been out of control. "What about it?"

His eyes held hers. Damn, but she was pulling him in. The worst thing in the world for a man in his position, for a man of his predisposition. But it was as if he were on the outside, watching himself do this. "I'd like to do something about that, too."

"A mercy lovemaking session?" she asked sarcastically.

His initial instinct brought denial to his lips. "I won't die without it." But then he relented. "But if you prefer thinking of it that way..." His voice trailed off.

She'd meant the bit about the mercy lovemaking session to refer to her, not him. His take on it surprised her. It also made him more human. "You're saying that you want it, too?"

He framed one side of her face with his hand. "I never do anything I don't want to do."

She thought of his comment when he'd appeared on the scene in the farmhouse. He'd seemed reluctant, despite the paid assignment. "Even rescuing me?"

Joshua smiled into her eyes. The woman didn't forget anything. "Even rescuing you. And we don't have to stand up."

Taking her by the hand, Joshua threaded his way around several tall, giant boxes with bold, foot-high black lettering on the side.

Against one wall there was enough space on the

floor for an average-size male to stretch out. He was a little taller than that, but it would do. Pausing, he stripped off his shirt and placed it on the floor.

"Not exactly a cape," he allowed. "But then Sir Walter Raleigh was dealing with a mud puddle. This is just dirt."

He had impressed her. She felt herself smiling despite efforts not to. "You do know how to improvise, Secret Agent Man."

Joshua winked at her, sending mini tidal waves through her stomach again. Holding her hand, he helped her down onto the floor. "I got an A in improvising in spy school."

Was that an inadvertent slip despite the humor? "Then you are a spy."

He lowered himself onto her, his hard body covering hers, creating anticipation. She felt her loins responding.

"I am if you want me to be."

"What I want you to be," she said, feeling her pulse accelerate to an incredible rate, "is here."

"I can do that."

Joshua pressed a kiss to her neck that began setting off all sorts of alarms inside her. Alarms she opted to ignore this one last time.

The rest of the clothes, per force, remained on, but that didn't diminish the explosions taking place within either one of them. Having to remain clothed heightened the sense of urgency as well as the sense of danger.

Joshua took possession of her like a man already familiar with the terrain, already invested with its ownership. Pru knew she should have been indignant, angry at his presumption. The only problem was she had the same sort of feeling about him. In her mind, she knew his body was merely on loan to her.

In her soul, however, it was a different matter. Her soul whispered that this could easily be forever. She pretended that she believed.

She curbed the desire to rip his trousers off, to shred them from his torso so that she could run her hands along his bare, hard body, thrilling to the taut muscles as well as to his biceps, triceps and pectorals. But if she did that, his pants would be in tatters, or close to it, and he couldn't very well go into the heart of London half-dressed. She could just see the headlines on the tabloids: Prime Minister's Daughter Making the Rounds with a Half-Naked Man.

The thought made her blood surge again. God, but it might be worth it.

"Hey, whoa, slow down," he said, laughing and then groaning because she'd almost brought him to a climax before he wanted to reach that destination. "We do have a little time to spare before the train hits the next station."

But Pru wasn't taking any chances. She'd already had too much time stolen from her, had learned not to take anything for granted. Especially this man, who seemed to draw out armed killers like flies to honey.

"Good," she murmured, splaying her hand along his muscles, skimming the tips of her nails along his chest as she twisted and turned beneath him. "Then we can do it twice."

His eyes smiled at her first. His lips were a bonus. "I'll do my best."

"That's all anyone can ask," she told him. Raising her head, she sealed her mouth to his. Trapping his very soul.

She made him feel like Superman. Able to leap tall buildings in a single bound. Make love nonstop until the world ended.

Joshua did what he could to keep his word and not disappoint her. The rhythmic clatter of the wheels absorbed the cries of pleasure that escaped her lips.

He couldn't get enough of her.

And when it was finally over and Pru laid panting beside him, her head cradled on his arm, he looked at her, trying not to think the thoughts that kept insisting on materializing. Thoughts he'd never entertained before about any woman.

Thoughts he shouldn't be entertaining now.

They belonged to two different worlds, worlds that would have never touched, had it not been for a violent act.

But she was here now, beside him, and there was no tomorrow, no next hour. There was only now.

Without thinking, he kissed her forehead. A sigh

escaped. And then he reined himself in. He was an agent of one of the most prestigious organizations in the world. He had to remember that.

To cover the tenderness, he pretended to laugh. "What the hell do they put into those granola bars?"

She smiled up at Joshua, feeling way too content now to shrink back and grasp hold of reality with both hands the way her survival instinct begged her to. It was all she could do to keep from going under for the third time. Because she wanted to make love again. And again. Until she expired.

Look at Pru the Shrew now, she thought. The afterglow took its time in leaving.

"I think the earth moved," she finally said, running her fingertip along his lips.

"Yeah."

Covering her hand with his own, he pressed her fingers to his lips and kissed them. Damn, he thought. Just damn.

"Me, too," he continued. "That's what happens when you make love on the floor of a freight car."

"I'll have to keep that in mind," Pru whispered.

She should be pulling herself together, getting ready to enter the city. Instead, she was hoping for a derailment that would keep them here indefinitely. Away from London and politics and everything else. She had to be insane.

As she watched, Joshua sat up, then rose to his feet. She wanted to linger, to let the moment continue and to keep all other moments, all other re-

alities, as far at bay as possible. But that was tanta-
mount to declaring that she would never grow up.
And she already had. After the euphoria slipped
away, no amount of pixie dust was going to ultimately make her feel safe.

Only Secret Agent Man seemed to know how to
accomplish that.

Twisting around, she followed him with her eyes.
"What are you doing?" she wanted to know when he
opened the door they'd originally used to get into
this car. Outside, trees appeared to be rushing by,
with the freight car standing still.

Illusion.

Maybe it was all an illusion, she thought. The way
she felt, the way her body hummed. Just an illusion.

Still, she clung to it.

"Checking to see how far along we are."

Pru felt as if she'd been nudged with a cattle prod
and scrambled to her feet. She'd almost forgotten
about their final destination. Making love with Joshua seemed to knock everything else out of her head.

From where she was, everything looked the same.
"You can do that?"

Her question amused him. Twelve hours ago, the
same question would have annoyed him. "Yes."

Picking up his shirt from the floor, she dusted it
off and then snaked her way over to him. How did
he know things like that, she wondered. Did he
look at the sky to get his bearings, the way sailors
used to?

With careful, measured steps, she made her way over to him, then inched her way forward and looked out. Looked like the middle of the forest to her. She held out his shirt to him, shaking the dirt out of it. "Here, you might need this to look civilized."

"Awful lot of responsibility for a piece of material." He grinned, shrugging into it. "Didn't know a shirt could do that."

She looked at him, struggling against the fond feelings that insisted on flooding through her. This was going to end very soon. Once he delivered her to Number 10 Downing Street, he'd go his way and she hers.

And never the twain shall meet.

She felt pain in the pit of her stomach.

"Well, maybe not in your case," she allowed, "but it does make you look a little more respectable." She straightened his collar, smoothing it down. "You'll want to look respectable when you meet my father."

He wondered if she meant picking up a jacket and tie from one of the shops once they were in London. "I have a feeling with all that's gone on in the last two days, he'd be happy to see me even if I was stark naked as long as I had you in tow."

Joshua was right, she thought. Prime minister or not, Jeremy Hill was still her father and he did love her. It was just the details of life that got in the way and separated them.

"Stark naked, huh?" she echoed, then shook her

head. "You're confusing my father with your lady friends." She looked out again just before he closed the door. "So how far are we going?"

"To the end of the line." The train was stationed near Canterbury.

She couldn't say why, but she liked the sound of that. To the end of the line. 'Til death do us part. She roused herself. Too far, her thoughts were going too far.

Pru cleared her throat. "How far away is that?"

He thought a second, envisioning the map he'd looked at and committed to memory before leaving. "Another thirty, forty kilometers, give or take."

She liked the sound of that. She'd be home soon.

And yet…

And yet it would mean that he would be out of her life. Like a comet streaking across the sky. A major force to be reckoned with one moment, gone without a trace the next.

She felt a deep pang in her chest.

But because she knew that was what he'd been charged with doing, she forced a smile to her lips. "Good, very good."

Joshua caught the minuscule difference in modulation. His was a very well-trained ear and he'd dabbled in profiling more than once.

"What's the matter?" As he asked, he took out his cell phone.

She didn't want to go into what was bothering her, why she wasn't rejoicing at the prospect of being delivered to her father's doorstep, safe and sound. So she changed the subject. Nodding at the phone, she asked, "Trying again?"

"Yes." He'd almost forgotten about phoning. One romp in the hay and he was behaving like some mindless dolt. That had never happened before.

And it wasn't going to happen again, he thought, putting himself on notice.

They had to have repaired the lines by now, he reasoned. Storm or no storm. But as he began to input the number to the prime minister's residence, he frowned. "Damn."

Turning, Pru glanced at the cell phone screen in Joshua's hand. "*Still* won't go through?"

He shook his head. The signal was back up, but that wasn't his problem. "Battery's down. It needs recharging. I had it on all evening, in case someone from the organization was trying to reach me and found a way to bypass the effects of the storm."

The "someone" he was thinking of was Lucia. The woman seemed to eat and sleep the Lazlo Group, even more than the rest of them.

And almost as much as his uncle did.

She craned her neck to see. There was still a faint bar running along the upper right-hand corner of the screen. "You've still got a little juice left," she pointed out.

Enough, he judged, to make one call, since calling was more draining than leaving the phone on. But as he resumed pushing buttons that would connect him to the prime minister, he was surprised when Pru took the phone from him.

"What are you doing?"

She held the phone like a trophy. "You might not be able to reach my father. If he's in a meeting, or in conference, he shuts off his phone and we slip into limbo. Uncle George never turns off his cell."

"Uncle George?" he repeated. Her dossier said nothing about an uncle. Both her parents and her stepmother were only children.

She nodded. "George Montgomery. He's my father's right-hand man, remember? Telling him I'm all right is as good as telling my father. Better. Because we'll be able to reach him."

The phone on the other end was actually ringing. She felt like cheering. And then the line was picked up. There was some crackling interference.

And then there was a deep, male voice answering. "Hello? Montgomery here."

Definitely time for cheering, she thought. It was over.

Chapter 14

Pru pressed the cell phone against her ear while covering the other one with her hand to mute the noise. "Uncle George, it's me, Pru."

There was shock in the voice on the other end. "Dear God, Pru, are you all right? We've all been so worried about you. What's that noise in the background?"

She was straining to hear his voice, hoping that the signal wouldn't abruptly disappear again. "That's the freight train."

"Freight train?" Montgomery echoed, sounding confused. "Where are you? Are you safe?"

Pru couldn't help glancing at Joshua, who was

standing very close to her as if he was trying to hear what was being said by the man she'd called. Safe was a matter of opinion, she thought. Physically, yes. In other ways, it remained to be seen.

She took a breath. "For now, yes. Tell my father I'm all right."

"Of course, of course. Tell me where you are and I'll send someone for you. Better yet, I'll come myself." *That* he heard, Pru thought, seeing the alerted look on Joshua's face. He signaled no, frowning.

It was against her better instincts to lie to Uncle George, but she didn't want to spend the rest of their short time together arguing with Joshua.

"It's much too complicated to explain right now, Uncle George. But tell my father I'll be there as soon as I can. Another couple of hours, maybe more. But definitely before the vote later today." That was the most important part. "Tell him to go ahead and vote his conscience. And that I'm proud of him." Something, she realized, that she had never said to her father before.

"I will," Montgomery promised. "But you're sure I can't—"

"I'm sure," she repeated reluctantly. "I—" There was crackling on the other end, and then nothing. "Uncle George? Uncle George, are you there?" When there was no response, Pru looked at the phone. The screen was completely blank, as if it hadn't been turned on. With a sigh, she flipped it closed and handed the cell phone to Joshua. "Your battery's dead." She tried to keep the irritation out of her voice. It seemed as if everything was conspiring against her. "You really should get a long-lasting one."

"It is." Joshua deposited the dead phone into his back pocket. "I haven't exactly been able to recharge it these past two days."

"Well, it's useless now." Still, she had managed to reach Uncle George, who'd tell her father that she'd escaped. Her father didn't have to worry about her anymore.

The train lunged, as if running over something small left on the tracks and she pitched forward against Joshua. He held her for a moment, then released her. A sharp jolt of electricity insisted on racing through her.

"Why wouldn't you let me tell Uncle George where we were? He could have sent a car to the next station to pick us up. We wouldn't have to continue the rest of this trip like excess parts of a tractor."

His explanation was simple. "Because we don't know who ordered your kidnapping."

That might be true, but there were some things that were a given. "Well, it wasn't George. He's like a second father to me. More," she amended, recalling a few traumatic moments when she was growing up, after her mother had died. "He was available to talk to when my father wasn't." She felt she owed it to the man to stand up for him. "I'd trust George Montgomery with my life."

Joshua looked unmoved. And unconvinced. "Right now your life is mine and I don't trust anyone with it."

She believed him. Pru sighed, frustrated. "How can you stand it?" she wanted to know. "Being like that? Not trusting anyone? Looking over your shoulder all the time?"

"I didn't say I didn't trust anyone. I trust the people I work with." They were a handpicked crew who answered to his uncle and met the man's rigid, high standards. He wouldn't hesitate to trust any of them. The rest of the world was suspect. And then he smiled at Pru. "And as for my life, it has its perks."

"Oh, right, I forgot. Hot and cold beautiful women running through your life twenty-four/seven," she noted sarcastically.

Joshua shook his head, amusement curving his lips. "I'm afraid you've watched too many James Bond movies."

There was a great deal of similarity between the fictional superagent and the man standing in front of her. More than she was happy about. "Your work takes you all around the world, correct?"

"Yes."

"And you never know where you're going to wake up tomorrow."

Where was she going with this, he wondered, amused at the determined expression on her face. "A slight exaggeration, but I'll give you the concept."

She continued as if he hadn't said anything. "And half the people you deal with are women."

He dealt more with men than with women, but he let that go. "Give or take."

"A little hard work, a little hard play, accomplish your mission and be on your way." That summed up his life, she thought. And made him someone whose life she didn't fit into.

His eyebrows drew together as he replayed her words in his head. "Did you just deliberately rhyme that?"

That did rhyme, didn't it? She hadn't realized that it would until the words had come out of her mouth. "No, but now that you mention it, I guess that could double as your theme song."

She had lost him entirely. He shook his head as if to clear it. "I'm sorry, but what is the point here?"

"At the top of my head it would seem." For allowing herself to dream, even for a moment, that there might be a possibility for some sort of relationship with him, other than the kind established by taking a number and queuing up.

He cocked his head and looked at her intently, trying to divine what she was actually saying. "Sam?"

She stared at him. "Who?"

Joshua laughed. "I asked you earlier what to call you and when I said 'Sam,' I believe your answer was 'whatever,' which I took as your acquiescence to it. For my part, I rather like it. At least I know that no one else will ever call you that."

And no one will ever make love to me the way you

did, either, she added silently. *But you probably already know that.*

"No, you have exclusive rights to that," she allowed.

He saw through her. "You're trying to change the subject."

Right now, her head felt as if it was in that fog they'd traveled through last night. She needed to pull herself together. "What subject?"

"I don't know, but if I read between the lines, you seem bent on making me out to be someone with no morals or scruples."

Was it her imagination, or was the car shaking more? She refrained from reaching for him to hang on to. *Can't let yourself get used to that,* she upbraided herself.

Pru shook her head. "Wrong. I know you have those. They might be a unique set, different from the average man on the street's scruples or morals, but you have them." She replayed what she'd just said and dropped her head into her hands. "Oh, God, now I'm babbling."

He slipped his arm around her. The journey was getting bumpier. "Perfectly normal, given what you've been through."

Pru stiffened, moving back. The sooner she separated herself from him, the better. "How much longer do you think it'll be before we reach London?"

He looked at her, amusement playing on his lips. "Are you that eager to get rid of me?"

It was a joke to him, she thought. Maybe even the last twenty-four hours had been a joke. "No," she said quietly, "I'm not." And then she lied. "Just eager to get a cold shower and a hot meal."

He nodded, accepting her excuse because it was plausible. "Not all that long. About two hours, like you told Montgomery. Except the train is going to Canterbury."

When had he decided this? Did he enjoy pulling strings, jerking her around like a puppet?

"Canterbury?" That was in the southeast. "I thought we were going straight to London."

"This train goes straight to Canterbury." Joshua held up the dead phone. "And since I can't reach my people, there's been a change of plans."

He didn't add that he wanted to reach Lazlo to alert him to the fact that at least one person in London knew the prime minister's daughter had escaped her captors. Until the bases were all covered, he'd have to take his own precautions. They were not home free yet.

Pru opened her mouth to protest that it didn't matter if he could reach his people or not as long as she physically reached hers. But then she shut it again. After all, if they weren't getting off at the London station, that meant she had that much more time to spend with him.

Before he was gone.

"Canterbury it is."

"You still haven't found him?"

The question preceded Corbett's entrance. He

strode into the work area that Lucia had, per force, temporarily taken over as she peeled away the layers of transmission that had reached his computer in the twenty-four-hour period before he had received the jarring communication.

She looked up from the screen, grateful for any diversion. Her eyes felt as if they were going crossed. "Who? The person who blew up Kiley? Or Joshua?"

He didn't expect her to read his mind but he did expect her to anticipate his requirements. "Both."

"No." When he looked at her, she clarified, "Neither one."

Corbett's frown seemed to go straight down to the bone. There were those at the group, when they found themselves on the receiving end, who still cowered inwardly. Lucia, after all these years, had become immune, knowing he rarely bit. "He should have called in by now."

"Joshua," she guessed.

"Yes, of course Joshua." His nephew never took advantage of their connection and had become, almost from the beginning, one of his most dependable operatives. If there was a way to have gotten in touch, Joshua would have found it.

He knew about the storm in the northern sector knocking out lines. But that problem had been attended to, plus Joshua's cell should be on. Why wasn't he checking in?

Lucia leaned back in her chair, turning it around

to fully face her employer. That was as close to snapping as she had ever heard him.

So, the man did have filial feelings, she thought. There were times when she was convinced that he was pure android, devoid of emotions, programmed to simultaneously oversee a multitude of projects, making sure they were all satisfactorily resolved. He was good at that, at juggling with both hands and feet without missing a beat. But most of his operatives thought him removed, lacking any feelings, good or bad.

They obviously thought wrong.

Treading lightly on the path that their long association had formed, she dared a personal remark. "He'll be all right, Lazlo. Joshua's a good agent."

"Of course he's a good agent. He's an excellent agent," he corrected as if it was a given. "I trained him. But there are times when even excellent agents are brought down."

Lucia read between the lines. "You're thinking of Kiley." Corbett made no reply. But he had to see that there were differences, she thought. "Kiley was finished with a case. She wasn't on her guard. Joshua's right in the middle of one right now. He's got eyes in the back of his head. Just like his mentor."

Corbett nodded at the screen in front of her, his meaning clear: Get back to work. "I'm not paying you to flatter me."

"Good," she answered sweetly, "because you couldn't pay me enough."

He began to leave. "Call me if you locate the bastard."

"The killer?"

Exasperated, he paused to turn on his heel. "Yes, the killer."

That was an actual flash of temper. He really had to be worried. He wasn't the only one. They weren't known for their failures, but there was always a first time and if this was it, the consequences would have international repercussions.

"Just so we're clear," she murmured, already turning back to the monitor. "You'll be the first to know."

She heard the door close behind her.

Pru savored the meal she had all but finished. Who would have ever thought a hamburger and fries could taste so good?

After sneaking off the freight train as it pulled into the station in Canterbury, Joshua had gotten them tickets on the next commuter train to London. They'd arrived within an hour.

She'd been surprised when his first move after getting them to London was taking her to a fast-food restaurant. She'd caught herself thinking that was just not his style. She saw him frequenting five-star restaurants, places that prided themselves on ambience, not speed.

Crumpling the wrapper that had held her burger, she licked the tips of her fingers. She had a weakness for salt.

When she saw him watching her, she dropped her hand into her lap. "I thought we were in a hurry."

"We are. But the vote's not for several hours and you said you were hungry." He'd ordered a hamburger himself, but hunger had only taken him so far and he left the second half on his tray. "What would the prime minister say if I brought you to him, bedraggled and starving?"

"I believe he'd say 'thanks.'" She smiled, taking a last sip of her soda. "My father is given to understatement." Pru wiped her mouth with her napkin, then dropped it on the tray. "Not very big on emotion, either."

"It's not a failing, you know."

His comment surprised her. "It's not exactly a deal clincher, either. Correct me if I'm wrong, but weren't you the one who gave me that big talk on the train about it being all right to feel?"

Amused, caught, he countered with his own question. "Do you remember everything?"

She grinned and nodded. "Annoyingly so." Her father had called it her annoying habit, especially when she called him on something that contradicted something else he'd told her earlier.

"So I'd better watch what I say around you."

As if that was going to be a problem, she thought. He made it sound as if they were going to continue being a part of each other's lives instead of the exact opposite. "Won't have to worry about that for too much longer," she told him.

Her words sobered him. He'd almost forgotten for a moment that she was his assignment and that he was bringing her home to her father.

"No, I don't suppose I will." There was one fry left, peeking out from the paper wrapper. "Finished?"

She popped the last fry into her mouth. "Just."

He rose to his feet, one hand holding the tray, one on her arm. "All right, let's get you some clothes." He dropped the tray on the collection stack on his way out.

She preceded him out the door. He appeared casual, but she saw the way he scanned the immediate area. Joshua was always on duty, she thought. "Have a sudden yen to play Henry Higgins, do you?"

He wasn't trying to change her. "You're not a 'guttersnipe,'" he pointed out, recalling the term that had been used to describe Eliza Dolittle. "But you do look a little too conspicuous like that." She looked down at her clothes, and then back at him uncertainly. "Every second person who walked by looked you over."

Ever since her father had become prime minister and the newspapers ran photographs of his family, she'd had to endure scrutiny like that. In a way, she'd become used to it. "Maybe they're trying to place me."

"Maybe." But he'd rather not have her recognized until after he brought her back. "In any case, I think you should get something to wear that involves a little more material."

He had a point. Her abdomen peeked out from

beneath the T-shirt she'd torn to bandage up his leg. Still, there was another way to interpret his words. "If I didn't know any better, I would say that you're jealous."

His expression never changed. "Cautious," he corrected.

She inclined her head. "Cautious." She liked her word better.

Joshua paid in cash, just as he'd paid for her lunch and the room at the inn the night before. He seemed to have an endless supply of money on him. She supposed that was where the term "deep pockets" originated.

"Don't you believe in credit cards?" she asked as they walked away from the saleswoman. He'd taken her to a huge department store where large purchases were the norm, but cash was not.

"I believe in not leaving a paper trail," he answered. "You use a credit card, you're instantly on the map."

She took a breath. His reasoning made her uneasy even though she pretended otherwise. "You really think someone is still out to get me?"

"Better safe than sorry, Sam."

She began to make a comment about the nickname, then changed her mind. She rather liked it, she decided, in an odd sort of way.

Leaving the department store in the pale green sheath and white high heels she'd exchanged for the sneakers, shorts and T-shirt she'd had on, Pru hooked her arm through his. "*Now* can I go see my father?"

That was why he'd been dispatched in the first place, he thought. "Yes."

He had an odd expression on his face just before he began to hail a cab. She moved so that she was in front of him again. "What?"

"Nothing." But she gave him a look that said she wasn't going to be satisfied with that kind of evasion. So he told her. "You clean up nicely, Sam."

For an international agent, that certainly wasn't a line that was guaranteed to turn a woman's head. But it warmed her nonetheless. "Thanks for noticing."

"I'd have to be blind not to," Joshua murmured, "and even then I'm not sure it wouldn't have registered somehow."

She felt her skin prickling. He made her want to make love with him right here, right now.

For a moment, she thought longingly of the dirty little room at the inn. Who would have ever thought that a flea-infested rattrap would have provided her with what was probably going to be one of her all-time favorite memories?

Joshua waved down a taxi, then peered into the interior at the driver and his posted license before deciding to make use of the man's services.

He opened the rear door for Pru and waited for her to get in, then slid in himself. "Number 10 Downing Street," he instructed, shutting the door.

The driver pulled down the meter flag. "Tourists?" he asked as he pulled away from the curb.

Pru was about to answer, then stopped as she felt the gentle pressure on her arm. He was doing it again, she thought, talking for her. Did he expect her to give the driver her life history? She knew when to keep quiet.

"Yes," Joshua answered with just a hint of an Australian accent. She looked at him but his expression was the soul of innocence.

"Not much to see at Number 10," the driver commented. "Tower of London, now there's an interesting place. Crawling with history. Ghosts, too, they say."

Joshua nodded, as if considering the suggestion. "Maybe later."

The driver shrugged his wide shoulders. "Your money."

The ride was short and uneventful. The driver kept his radio on loud. Despite the distracting noise, Joshua remained on his guard throughout. Did he ever relax? she wondered. And then she laughed at her own question, remembering the motel room and the ride on the freight train. He had his own way of relaxing, she supposed.

"We'll get out here," Joshua said suddenly as they approached Whitehall Street.

The driver turned to look at him, puzzled. "But Number 10's a block away."

"That's all right, we'll walk. Stop the cab," he ordered more forcefully.

There was such a thing as being too paranoid, Pru thought, getting out.

There was a fence, constructed in 1989, on the Whitehall end of Downing. Looking down the street, she thought she saw Uncle George. She blinked once, focusing. The man was standing not too far from the side entrance to the gardens. He looked as if he were waiting for someone.

It was him. It was George Montgomery.

Suddenly, she just wanted to hug him, to touch someone from her life and make the connection that she was actually home.

Joshua realized what she was doing half a second after she left his side. Looking up the street, he saw the man she was running toward. The man who had been in the room when he'd talked with the prime minister.

"Damn it." Digging into his pocket, Joshua was about to toss a fistful of bills at the driver and take off after her when he heard something on the radio that caught his attention.

Chapter 15

The words that he'd just heard on the taxi's radio still echoed in his head. Joshua tried to move fast, but his wound was giving him trouble again. He couldn't run the way he was capable of under normal circumstances.

"Sam, wait up! Stop."

But Pru didn't. Not until she'd almost reached the man she'd been calling "Uncle George" since she was five years old. Even after she'd been told that he was not an actual blood relation, but her father's college roommate and one of his closest friends, she'd continued referring to Montgomery that way. Because he was like family.

Tall, distinguished-looking, with gray hair and kind, brown eyes, Montgomery now acted as one of the prime minister's advisors. His chief advisor, actually. But George was so much more. He'd been the one who had helped her get her present apartment when she had agreed to give up her position with the Red Cross in Africa and move back to London. Moreover, he'd been instrumental in healing the rift that had sprung up between her and her father. She'd been maid of honor at his only daughter's wedding last year. Not to trust Uncle George was not to trust anyone.

But there was something about Joshua's tone, about his voice, that almost compelled her to halt in her tracks. So she finally did, within a few feet of George Montgomery. And just for a fleeting moment, she thought she saw something in the man's eyes, something that looked akin to regret.

An inexplicable chill surrounded her heart even as she tried to ignore it.

The older man crossed to her, melting the distance to nothing, and embracing her with his large, bearlike arms. "Pru, you're all right." There was relief in every syllable. And then he held her at arm's length, to look her over and assure himself that she truly was all right. "They didn't hurt you, did they?"

Pru merely shook her head, too overcome with emotion, with anger and with confusion at the ambivalent feelings that had momentarily sprung up, then vanished, to speak. The turmoil she was feeling was all because of Lazlo, because of the seeds of doubt he'd planted.

She was angry at him for that, for making her distrust one of the few staples in her life: that George Montgomery was a good and kind man who could be trusted with anything.

Embracing her one more time, Montgomery looked over Pru's head at the man who came to join them. "I don't know how we can thank you for bringing our Pru back to us."

Our Pru. How could she distrust him? she thought bitterly.

Releasing her, Montgomery slipped an arm around Pru's shoulders. "Let's go inside, Pru, before we attract one of those damn photographers who always seemed to be hounding you." But when Joshua fell into step with them, Montgomery slowed and shook his head. "No need for you to come along, Mr. Lazlo," he informed him kindly, his deep resonant voice sounding forceful. "Your services are no longer needed."

"If you don't mind," Joshua said pleasantly, although his tone didn't fool Pru, "I'll just tag along. The assignment's not over until I hand the subject over to the client who hired me."

Montgomery hesitated, although he continued walking with Pru toward the side entrance that led to 10 Downing Street's garden.

"I assure you, you will be well compensated for what you've done." His voice grew in strength as he made his point. "But her father would like to see her alone. You understand, don't you? He wants a private moment." Pausing, Montgomery looked down at Pru. "You might think him an unemotional man, Pru, but your father has been through hell over this and I know he wouldn't want his first moments with you witnessed by a stranger."

"So you told him that his daughter was safe," Joshua assumed.

Almost at the gate's entrance, Montgomery looked at him indignantly. "Of course I told the prime minister. I told him she'd escaped the moment I received Pru's phone call. You really should have told me where you were. I could have had you here sooner," he told Pru.

But Joshua wedged himself in between Pru and the advisor. "Then why did the newscaster on the radio just say that the prime minister had surprised his party by throwing his lot in with the faction opposing sanctions against Naessa?"

Pru's eyes narrowed as she turned to look at Joshua. What was he talking about? How would he know something like that? "When did you—?"

Joshua never took his eyes off Montgomery. "Just now, when I was paying the driver." He pointed vaguely behind him where they'd gotten out. "He had on the radio. When you ran out, a news bulletin was just coming on about the prime minister's un-expected announcement. He'd made it in hopes of communicating with the kidnappers. The kidnappers he thought still had you." Joshua moved Pru behind him as he spoke. "You were the only one Pru told she was free. She charged you with telling her father. But you didn't tell him, did you, Mr. Montgomery?"

Uneasiness clawed at her throat as she looked at George, willing him to come up with a plausible explanation. She didn't want to believe what Joshua was saying. "Uncle George?"

Suddenly, Montgomery grabbed Pru's arm and pulled her to him. She saw that there was a small pistol in his hand. With his back to the street, no one could see what he was holding, or that he had the gun pressed to her side.

Pru felt as if she'd just been stabbed.

"God forgive me, Pru, I didn't want it to come to this, I truly didn't. They swore to me they wouldn't hurt you. I just needed you to stay out of the way until the vote was taken."

She looked up at him, pale, livid. Hurt beyond words. "And then what, pretend this never happened? Keep your part in this a secret? How, Uncle George?" she demanded. "How were you going to do that?"

"You weren't supposed to know I ordered the kidnapping. Pru, if your father does this thing, if he puts his weight behind the bill bringing sanctions against Naessa, it'll pass. And everything I own will turn to ashes." He was pleading with her to understand. "Every penny I have is in those factories in

Naessa. Relations break down, those factories will be nationalized and I'll be ruined." There was almost a sob in that strong, resonant voice. It twisted her heart to hear it. "And Bethany will leave me."

"Your wife?" Her eyes widened. As much as she loved George Montgomery, that was how much she disliked Bethany Montgomery. The woman was shallow and materialistic. She'd even seen the woman, shortly after her father was widowed, flirt with her father outrageously in hopes, no doubt, of marrying her way up the ladder.

Pru'd never seen a smile as sad as the one that now curved Montgomery's mouth. It twisted her heart. "The care and feeding of whom I have been attending to all these years. Do you think a woman like that would have remained with a second-class man like me if I wasn't constantly showering her with everything her heart desired?"

Pru was speechless and numb. And felt horribly betrayed.

Joshua took advantage of the lull to demand, "Who's behind this, Montgomery? Who did you go to to arrange this?"

The prime minister's chief advisor looked like a man trapped. A man who had nowhere to turn and yet desperately sought to find that one small chink in the wall, that crack that would allow him to slip through and make his way to safety.

"If I told you that," Montgomery replied, "then I would not only be ruined, I'd be dead. Believe me when I tell you that their reach is very long. It spans entire continents."

Joshua knew of only one group that warranted that sort of description. For the time being, he didn't mention a name. But he did offer a promise.

"We'll protect you," Joshua told him. Out of the corner of his eye, he saw the surprised look on Pru's face. She'd obviously thought he was going to tell the man to turn himself in.

Montgomery shook his head sadly. "Night and day? For the rest of my life?"

Joshua did not waver in his conviction. His uncle had resources that could be used. "If need be."

For a moment, Montgomery looked tempted. But then he shook his head again. "Moot point. Without Bethany, I'd rather be dead anyway."

A single shot suddenly rang out. The next second, George Montgomery crumpled at Pru's feet. She screamed at the exact same moment that Joshua threw himself over her. His weapon was instantly in his hand as he scanned the immediate area for the shooter.

There were no more shots. The target had been acquired and taken down.

Her head throbbing, Pru heard the sound of voices in the distance, calling. Heard the sound of running feet hitting the pavement. Coming toward them.

She didn't look up, didn't look in their direction. All she could do was look at the man whose blood was oozing so freely onto the hard concrete beneath him.

This wasn't happening!

She wanted to seal his wound with her fingers, but it was too big, the blood was flowing too fast. She lowered her face to Montgomery's so that he could hear her as she wrapped her hand around his, trying to tether him to this world and keep him from entering the next. "Uncle George, hang on, help's coming."

His resonant voice was thin, reedy. Barely audible. "Too late...too late." His eyes shifted to her face, the light fading. "Forgive...me...Pru."

"Who did this to you?" Joshua demanded. "Give me a name."

But in the last moments of his life, the man who had always come in second to his best friend looked at the only person who mattered. "Pru?"

Tears choked her throat. "I forgive you, Uncle George, but only if you hang on. Only if you live. Please," she begged.

But it was already too late.

Drained, Pru felt someone raising her to her feet. And then someone was gently holding her. "He's gone, Sam."

Something felt as if it broke inside her.

And then she heard her father's voice, brimming with emotion. "Prudence! Prudence! Oh, dear God, Prudence, you're alive. You're alive."

The next moment, Joshua was stepping back, allowing Prime Minister Hill, who had just been informed of what was happening on the north side of the garden, clear access to his oldest daughter. The older man quickly swept her into his arms for a long, soulful embrace as his bodyguards closed ranks around all three of them. Several others immediately attended to George Montgomery.

"Hi, Dad," she said brightly, trying her best to keep a tight rein on her own vulnerable emotions. "So, did you miss me?"

"Stop it, Prudence. No more pretenses," her father ordered sternly. She would have taken offense had there not been tears shimmering in his eyes. The sight of them instantly set off her own.

"Okay, Dad, no more pretenses." And with that, she melted into her father's arms, the way she used to when she was a child.

It was only after several minutes had passed that the prime minister looked at Joshua and then down at the body of his best friend. His voice was tight, shaken, as he asked, "What happened?"

Joshua never hesitated. "I rescued your daughter from her abductors yesterday. We were just coming to 10 Downing Street when another attempt was made on her life. Mr. Montgomery shielded her with his body before I was able to. He gave his life to save hers," he added with feeling.

The prime minister made no attempt to wipe away the tears that were now falling freely. He'd just lost his best friend and regained his daughter all in the space of a few seconds.

"Most precious gift George ever gave me," Hill

said, his voice filled with emotion. The prime minister drew himself up, one arm still firmly around his daughter's shoulders. "George Montgomery will have the finest funeral the realm can give him, with all the honors he deserves."

Pru nodded, avoiding Joshua's eyes. Remembering all the good and willing herself to forget the bad. "He would be very pleased."

"Why did you do that?" Pru asked Joshua later that evening.

They had left Number 10 Downing Street several hours ago. The commotion had died down, the vote on the bill in question had been taken and her father had been free to follow his conscience. Ironically, when the bill passed, her father vowed to make up for the loss of monies because of the severed ties with Naessa. Bethany Montgomery would continue being a wealthy woman, the way she always wanted. The only difference being that she was now a wealthy widow.

That, too, possibly, would be to her liking, Pru thought, struggling to keep her feelings in check. George's betrayal cut deep—too deep for her to deal with right now. Right now, she just wanted to remember him the way he'd been to her, growing up. Kind, with integrity. "Why did you lie to my father about Uncle George?"

He leaned back in his chair. They were on her terrace, overlooking the city. He'd done his duty, calling in to Lucia and reporting all the pertinent details. The group, still in upheaval over Kiley's murder, were now busy trying to find who it was that Montgomery had sought out to handle Pru's abduction. His uncle, Lucia told him, thought there was a connection.

Toying with the tall, frosty drink in his hand, Joshua shrugged. "Didn't see the point in besmirching an otherwise spotless record."

Her mouth curved. Now there was a word she hadn't heard in a very long time. "Besmirching?"

"Good word, not used nearly often enough," he commented before taking another long sip. Placing his glass on the small circular table between them, he looked up at the sky.

All that vastness. Made a man feel small, he mused.

He had to have more of a reason than that, Pru thought. He hardly knew the advisor. "Aren't you supposed to tell the truth, the whole truth, and nothing but the truth, so help you God?"

He laughed at the words she used. "I wasn't under oath."

He knew what she meant, Pru thought, feeling unaccountably irritated. "Don't you swear one when you set out?"

There'd been no spoken oaths, no papers signed when he joined the group. Things were understood. "I tell the truth when it's prudent, and a lie when I feel it's justified and necessary. George Montgomery did a stupid thing because he loved too much. He'd already paid the ultimate price, no reason to make his daughter pay." He glanced back at Pru. "Your best friend, right?"

She shifted, feeling somewhat uncomfortable. She hated it when the scales weren't balanced. "Do you know everything there is about me?"

"Pretty much." He took another sip, then retired the now empty glass. "And what I didn't know, I learned."

As far as time went, they hadn't been together much longer than the life span of a fruit fly. Most of that was spent running. Not exactly the perfect atmosphere to acquire any kind of knowledge.

"Such as?" she challenged.

He grinned then. "Such as you have a very attractive mole just on the inside of your—"

"Never mind where that is." Pru rose to her feet and crossed the short distance to the railing. Folding her hands before her as she leaned them on the railing, she looked out into the city. There were lights everywhere. She felt only darkness. "So, Secret Agent Man, when do you say goodbye?"

He rose to join her. "Usually when I walk out the door."

She made an impatient noise. "To me, when do you say goodbye to me?"

He skimmed his fingertips along the back of her neck. "Trying to get rid of me?"

"No. Yes." It was hard not sinking into the sensation he was creating. But he was trying to distract her and she knew it. Pru swung around. "Damn it, Lazlo, you confuse the hell out of me."

The grin softened into a smile. "I like it better when you call me Secret Agent Man. There's a certain light in your eyes when you do."

Damn it, her heart rate was beginning to speed up. He was getting to her. Was there going to be one last bedding before he was on his way? Her pride called for her to resist, the rest of her was begging otherwise. She took a long breath.

"That was when we were running for our lives. We're back now."

He drew a little closer to her. "What makes you think you're safe?"

Her eyes widened even as she felt the rest of her anticipating things she shouldn't. "I'm not?"

Joshua's voice was dead serious. "There's always an outside chance that someone else might try to abduct you. I heard your father talking about hiring a three-man team."

When had that happened? She shut her eyes and groaned. "Oh, God."

"Fortunately for you," he continued, "I convinced him you'd never stand for it."

She didn't know if he was serious or not, but knowing her father, there was a very good chance that the topic had been brought up. "Thank you."

Joshua wasn't finished yet. "I suggested using only one."

"One?" One, twelve, it was all the same. An invasion of her life. She just couldn't deal with that. "One shadow, one spook, one man poking his nose where it doesn't belong?"

He stopped her before she could go off and running. "Depends on if you think I don't belong."

That brought her to a grinding halt. For a second, she clamped down her mouth. When she opened it again, there was only a single word. "You?"

He nodded. "Unofficially."

That didn't make any sense. Operatives of the Lazlo Group weren't bodyguards indefinitely, officially or unofficially. "But you already have a job. You're with the organization, or company, or group or whatever it is they call themselves."

He had no intentions of leaving the group at the present time. Being an operative was who and what he was. But that no longer meant he couldn't broaden his parameters. "A man has to remain gainfully employed in order to support a wife."

"A wife?" She stared at him, stunned. "You have a wife?" And then blind fury set in. He'd strung her along. Lied to her. Made her feel things. She could have cut out his heart. "You son of a bitch, you have a wife and you didn't say anything?"

He grabbed her wrists just as she started to take a swing at him. Holding them both tightly, he caught her up against him. "I didn't say anything because I don't have a wife. Yet."

He wasn't making any sense. "So, what? She's coming in the mail?" she asked sarcastically.

Joshua laughed, refusing to release her even though she was tugging in earnest. "Only if you fit into the slot."

Pru stopped tugging. Stopped breathing. "Me?"

He stood there for a moment, just looking at her. The moonlight was weaving its way through her hair, lightly caressing her face. He'd had a great many women in his life. Shadow women. Women of beauty but no substance. Prudence Hill had substance enough for two-and-a-half women. Maybe three. There'd be no dull moments with her, no lulls in conversations, drifting aimlessly into awkward silence. Silence with her, though rare he was confident, would be comfortable. He sensed it without being told.

Just as he sensed that this was the one woman for him.

"Yes, you," he said quietly, releasing her wrists and instead taking her hands in his. "Who did you think I meant?"

She shrugged. "Some addle-brained woman who's willing to put up with a husband who moves in and out of her life like some gray ghost."

He searched her face for a clue to her true feelings. "Are you turning me down?"

She lifted her chin defiantly. "How can I turn down what's never been asked?"

All right, he'd make it formal. "Will you marry me, Sam?"

"We've only known each other a day," she protested, even though the romanticism of it did secretly thrill her.

He had her dossier, and he'd been in her company for a very harrowing number of hours. It had made up his mind for him. "I know all I need to know, and we'll have the rest of our lives together to learn the rest."

She shook her head. "You're crazy, you know that?"

"That's beside the point." He slipped his arms around her, pulling her close to him. "You're evading the question."

She sighed, weaving her arms around his neck. "I guess I'm crazy, too."

He grinned. "The kids are going to be a handful."

She pulled back, looking at him sharply. Were there children he wasn't telling her about? "What kids?"

"Ours."

She relaxed. The thought of having children with this man suddenly pleased her. "I'm up to it."

"I never doubted it for a second," he told her just before he brought his mouth down to hers.

Epilogue

Lucia swept into Corbett's office.

Tension seemed to crackle with every step she took. The atmosphere had been like that for the past several weeks. Ever since Jane Kiley had been taken out. Everyone at the Lazlo Group had been on heightened alert even though, to the untrained eye, it appeared to be business as usual.

Lost in thought, Corbett looked up as Lucia approached his desk. His eyes went to the folder she held against her.

"I've tapped into Montgomery's phone logs," she announced. "All of them. At his office, his home, his personal cell."

It took some doing. Even a group like his had rules that had to be attended to. Lazlo knew she'd worked hard. "And?"

"And I think I might have an answer as to who Montgomery had gotten in contact with to pull off the abduction." She paused for a moment. "You're not going to like it."

Impatience creased his brow. Whenever possible, Corbett appreciated having his information presented cut-and-dried.

"When did you get this flair for drama?"

Lucia allowed herself a smile. "A girl has to do something to amuse herself." She placed the pages in question, gleaned after trolling through reams of others, in front of him on his desk.

He looked at the circled phone numbers, knowing there was more. "And this traces back to?"

"An old friend. Or enemy, depending on your viewpoint," she amended.

It was Lucia's moment and she was drawing it out. He knew she received precious little recognition even though he had no doubt that a great part of his operation would grind to a halt without her talents.

Still, he wasn't feeling very magnanimous at the moment. All morning he'd been fighting this feeling that something was wrong.

"I'm not in the mood for games, Lucia. Joshua's taken off on holiday—"

Her mouth curved. Only he would be that dismissive of his operatives' private lives. "They still call it a honeymoon, I believe."

"Whatever." His tone bordered on exasperation. "With Kiley gone that leaves us without two of our key operatives. The ones in training are still too green to bring up—"

"In your opinion," she pointed out.

He raised his eyes to hers. His was the only opinion that mattered in this case. "Must you contradict everything I say?"

"No, not everything," she allowed cheerfully. "Just—"

Lucia didn't get a chance to finish. A soft bell sounded, announcing another e-mail's arrival on his desktop.

Lazlo retreated to his computer with Lucia directly behind him. Hitting a key to bring up the message, he experienced a feeling of déjà vu. There was a single line across his screen.

Ready for round 2?

The phone behind him began to ring.

* * * * *

The Lazlo Group is under fire!
Don't miss the next thrilling story
in the Mission: Impassioned *continuity,*
SECRET AGENT REUNION
by Caridad Piñeiro,
on sale in August 2006 wherever
Silhouette Books are sold.

Award-winning author Stevi Mittman delivers
another hysterical mystery, featuring Teddi
Bayer, an irrepressible heroine, and her to-die-
for hero, Detective Drew Scoones. After all,
life on Long Island can be murder!

*Turn the page for a sneak peek at the warm and
funny fourth book,
WHOSE NUMBER IS UP, ANYWAY?,
in the Teddi Bayer series,
by STEVI MITTMAN.
On sale August 7.*

CHAPTER 1

"Before redecorating a room, I always advise my
clients to empty it of everything but one chair.
Then I suggest they move that chair from place
to place, sitting in it, until the placement feels
right. Trust your instincts when deciding on fur-
niture placement. Your room should "feel right."
—TipsFromTeddi.com

Gut feelings. You know, that gnawing in the pit of
your stomach that warns you that you are about to
do the absolute stupidest thing you could do? Something that will ruin life as you know it?

I've got one now, standing at the butcher counter in King Kullen, the grocery store in the same strip mall as L.I. Lanes, the bowling alley cum billiard parlor I'm in the process of redecorating for its "Grand Opening."

I realize being in the wrong supermarket probably doesn't sound exactly dire to you, but you aren't the one buying your father a brisket at a store your mother will somehow know isn't Waldbaum's.

And then, June Bayer isn't your mother.

The woman behind the counter has agreed to go into the freezer to find a brisket for me, since there aren't any in the case. There are packages of pork tenderloin, piles of spare ribs and rolls of sausage, but no briskets.

Warning Number Two, right? I should be so out of here.

But no, I'm still in the same spot when she comes back out, brisketless, her face ashen. She opens her mouth as if she is going to scream, but only a gurgle comes out.

And then she pinballs out from behind the counter, knocking bottles of Peter Luger Steak Sauce to the floor on her way, now hitting the tower of cans at the end of the prepared foods aisle and sending them sprawling, now making her way down the aisle, careening from side to side as she goes.

Finally, from a distance, I hear her shout, "He's deeeeeeaaaad! Joey's deeeeeaaaad."

My first thought is *You should always trust your gut.*

My second thought is that now, somehow, my mother will know I was in King Kullen. For weeks I will have to hear "What did you expect?" as though whenever you go to King Kullen someone turns up dead. And if the detective investigating the case turns out to be Detective Drew Scoones…well, I'll never hear the end of that from her, either.

She still suspects I murdered the guy who was found dead on my doorstep last Halloween just to get Drew back into my life.

Several people head for the butcher's freezer and I position myself to block them. If there's one thing I've learned from finding people dead—and the guy on my doorstep wasn't the first one—it's that the police get very testy when you mess with their murder scenes.

"You can't go in there until the police get here," I say, stationing myself at the end of the butcher's counter and in front of the Employees Only door, acting as if I'm some sort of authority. "You'll contaminate the evidence if it turns out to be murder."

Shouts and chaos. You'd think I'd know better than to throw the word *murder* around. Cell phones are flipping open and tongues are wagging.

I amend my statement quickly. "Which, of course, it probably isn't. Murder, I mean. People die all the time, and it's not always in hospitals or their own beds, or…" I babble when I'm nervous, and the idea of someone dead on the other side of the freezer door makes me very nervous.

So does the idea of seeing Drew Scoones again. Drew and I have this on-again, off-again sort of thing…that I kind of turned off.

Who knew he'd take it so personally when he tried to get serious and I responded by saying we could talk about *us* tomorrow—and then caught a plane to my parents' condo in Boca the next day? In July. In the middle of a job.

For some crazy reason, he took that to mean that I was avoiding him and the subject of *us*.

That was three months ago. I haven't seen him since.

The manager, who identifies himself and points to his nameplate in case I don't believe him, says he has to go into *his cooler.* "Maybe Joey's not dead," he says. "Maybe he can be saved, and you're letting him die in there. Did you ever think of that?"

In fact, I hadn't. But I had thought that the murderer might try to go back in to make sure his tracks were covered, so I say that I will go in and check.

Which means that the manager and I couple up and go in together while everyone pushes against the doorway to peer in, erasing any chance of finding clean prints on that Employee Only door.

I expect to find carcasses of dead animals hanging from hooks, and maybe Joey hanging from one, too. I think it's going to be very creepy and I steel myself, only to find a rather benign series of shelves with large slabs of meat laid out carefully on them, along with boxes and boxes marked simply Chicken.

Nothing scary here, unless you count the body of a middle-aged man with graying hair sprawled faceup on the floor. His eyes are wide open and unblinking. His shirt is stiff. His pants are stiff. His body is stiff. And his expression, you should forgive the pun—is frozen. Bill-the-manager crosses himself and stands mute while I pronounce the guy dead in a sort of *happy now?* tone.

"We should not be in here," I say, and he nods his head emphatically and helps me push people out of the doorway just in time to hear the police sirens and see the cop cars pull up outside the big store windows.

Bobbie Lyons, my partner in Teddi Bayer Interior Designs (and also my neighbor, my best friend and my private fashion police), and Mark, our carpenter (and my dogsitter, confidant, and ego booster), rush in from next door. They beat the cops by a half step and shout out my name. People point in my direction.

After all the publicity that followed the unfortunate incident during which I shot my ex-husband, Rio Gallo, and then the subsequent murder of my first client—which I solved, I might add—it seems like the whole world, or at least all of Long Island, knows who I am.

Mark asks if I'm all right. (Did I remember to mention that the man is drop-dead-gorgeous-but-a-decade-too-young-for-me-yet-too-old-for-my-daughter-thank-God?) I don't get a chance to answer him because the police are quickly closing in on the store manager and me.

"The woman—" I begin telling the police. Then I have to pause for the manager to fill in her name, which he does: *Fran.*

I continue. "Right. Fran. Fran went into the freezer to get a brisket. A moment later she came out and screamed that Joey was dead. So I'd say she was the one who discovered the body."

"And you are…?" the cop asks me. It comes out a bit like who do I *think* I am, rather than who am I really?

"An innocent bystander," Bobbie, hair perfect, makeup just right, says, carefully placing her body between the cop and me.

"And she was just leaving," Mark adds. They each take one of my arms.

Fran comes into the inner circle surrounding the cops. In case it isn't obvious from the hairnet and bloodstained white apron with Fran embroidered on it, I explain that she was the butcher who was going for the brisket. Mark and Bobbie take that as a signal that I've done my job and they can now get me out of there. They twist around, with me in the middle, as if we're a Rockettes line, until we are facing away from the butcher counter. They've managed to propel me a few steps toward the exit when disaster—in the form of a Mazda RX7 pulling up at the loading curb—strikes.

Mark's grip on my arm tightens like a vise. "Too late," he says.

Bobbie's expletive is unprintable. "Maybe there's a back door," she suggests, but Mark is right. It's too late.

I've laid my eyes on Detective Scoones. And while my gut is trying to warn me that my heart shouldn't go there, regions farther south are melting at just the sight of him.

"Walk," Bobbie orders me.

And I try to. Really.

Walk, I tell my feet. *Just put one foot in front of the other*.

I can do this because I know, in my heart of hearts, that if Drew Scoones was still interested in me, he'd have gotten in touch with me after I returned from Boca. And he didn't.

Since he's a detective, Drew doesn't have to wear one of those dark blue Nassau County Police uniforms. Instead, he's got on jeans, a tight-fitting T-shirt and a tweedy sports jacket. If you think that sounds good, you should see him. Chiseled features, cleft chin, brown hair that's naturally a little sandy in the front, a smile that…well, that doesn't matter. He isn't smiling now.

He walks up to me, tucks his sunglasses into his breast pocket and looks me over from head to toe.

"Well, if it isn't Miss Cut and Run," he says. "Aren't you supposed to be somewhere in Florida or something?" He looks at Mark accusingly, as if he was covering for me when he told Drew I was gone.

"Detective Scoones?" one of the uniforms says.

"The stiff's in the cooler and the woman who found him is over there." He jerks his head in Fran's direction.

Drew continues to stare at me.

You know how when you were young, your mother always told you to wear clean underwear in case you were in an accident? And how, a little farther on, she told you not to go out in hair rollers because you never knew who you might see—or who might see you? And how now your best friend says she wouldn't be caught dead without makeup and suggests you shouldn't either?

Okay, today, *finally,* in my overalls and Converse sneakers, I get it.

I brush my hair out of my eyes. "Well, I'm back," I say. As if he hasn't known my exact whereabouts. The man is a detective, for heaven's sake. "Been back awhile."

Bobbie has watched the exchange and apparently decided she's given Drew all the time he deserves. "And we've got work to do, so…" she says, grabbing my arm and giving Drew a little two-fingered wave goodbye.

As I back up a foot or two, the store manager sees his chance and places himself in front of Drew, trying to get his attention. Maybe what makes Drew such a good detective is his ability to focus.

Only what he's focusing on is me.

"Phone broken? Carrier pigeon died?" he asks me, taking in Fran, the manager, the meat counter and that Employees Only door, all without taking his eyes off me.

Mark tries to break the spell. "We've got work to do there, you've got work to do here, Scoones," Mark says to him, gesturing toward next door. "So it's back to the alley for us."

Drew's lip twitches. "You working the alley now?" he says.

"If you'd like to follow me," Bill-the-manager, clearly exasperated, says to Drew—who doesn't respond. It's as if waiting for my answer is all he has to do.

So, fine. "You knew I was back," I say.

The man has known my whereabouts every hour of the day for as long as I've known him. And my mother's not the only one who won't buy that he "just happened" to answer this particular call. In fact, I'm willing to bet my children's lunch money that he's taken every call within ten miles of my home since the day I got back.

And now he's gotten lucky.

"*You* could have called *me*," I say.

"You're the one who said *tomorrow* for our talk and then flew the coop, chickie," he says. "I figured the ball was in your court."

"Detective?" the uniform says. "There's something you ought to see in here."

Drew gives me a look that amounts to *in or out?*

He could be talking about the investigation, or about our relationship.

Bobbie tries to steer me away. Mark's fists are balled. Drew waits me out, knowing I won't be able to resist what might be a murder investigation.

Finally he turns and heads for the cooler.

And, like a puppy dog, I follow.

Bobbie grabs the back of my shirt and pulls me to a halt.

"I'm just going to show him something," I say, yanking away.

"Yeah," Bobbie says, pointedly looking at the buttons on my blouse. The two at breast level have popped. "That's what I'm afraid of."

HARLEQUIN®

Mediterranean NIGHTS™

Glamour, elegance, mystery and revenge aboard the high seas...

Coming in August 2007...

THE TYCOON'S SON

by
award-winning author
Cindy Kirk

Businessman Theo Catomeris's long-estranged father is determined to reconnect with his son, so he hires Trish Melrose to persuade Theo to renew his contract with Liberty Line. Sailing aboard the luxurious *Alexandra's Dream* is a rare opportunity for the single mom to mix business and pleasure. But an undeniable attraction between Trish and Theo is distracting her from the task at hand....

HARLEQUIN®

Super Romance®

*Looking for a romantic, emotional
and unforgettable escape?*

*You'll find it this month and every month
with a Harlequin Superromance!*

Rory Gorenzi has a sense of humor and a sense of
honor. She also happens to be good with children.

Seamus Lee, widower and father of four, needs
someone with exactly those traits.

They meet at the Colorado mountain school owned
by Rory's father, where she teaches skiing and
avalanche safety. But Seamus—and his children—
learn more from her than that....

Look for

GOOD WITH CHILDREN

by Margot Early,

*available August 2007, and these other
fantastic titles from Harlequin Superromance.*

Silhouette® *Desire*

REASONS FOR REVENGE

A brand-new provocative miniseries by *USA TODAY* bestselling author **Maureen Child** begins with

SCORNED BY THE BOSS

Jefferson Lyon is a man used to having his own way. He runs his shipping empire from California, and his admin Caitlyn Monroe runs the rest of his world. When Caitlin decides she's had enough and needs new scenery, Jefferson devises a plan to get her back. Jefferson *never* loses, but little does he know that he's in a competition....

Don't miss any of the other titles from the REASONS FOR REVENGE trilogy by *USA TODAY* bestselling author **Maureen Child**.

SCORNED BY THE BOSS #1816
Available August 2007

SEDUCED BY THE RICH MAN #1820
Available September 2007

CAPTURED BY THE BILLIONAIRE #1826
Available October 2007

Only from Silhouette Desire!

REQUEST YOUR FREE BOOKS!

2 FREE NOVELS PLUS 2 FREE GIFTS!

Silhouette® Romantic

SUSPENSE

Sparked by Danger, Fueled by Passion!

Romantic

SUSPENSE

COMING NEXT MONTH

#1475 HIGH-STAKES HONEYMOON—RaeAnne Thayne
Olivia Lambert is having one hell of a honeymoon. As if being groomle
wasn't bad enough, now she's been kidnapped by a handsome stranger
claiming there's a ransom for her life! How is she supposed to trust a m.
she just met, a man who has threatened her and dragged her across the
open ocean—a man who stirs a desire she never felt before?

#1476 SECRET AGENT REUNION—Caridad Piñeiro
Mission: Impassioned
A mysterious betrayal led super spy Danielle Moore to fake her own
death. Now she is ready to re-emerge and seek vengeance. But things ge
complicated when she realizes a mole in her agency is still leaking vital
information—and her new partner is the ex-lover she thought dead.

#1477 THE MEDUSA AFFAIR—Cindy Dees
The Medusa Project
When Misty Cordell hears a distress call over her radio, little does she
realize a three-hour flight is about to turn into the adventure of a lifetime
"Greg" Harkov has been leading a double life as a spy for too long and
discovers Misty could be his key out. But can he trust her with his life…
and his heart?

#1478 DANGER AT HER DOOR—Beth Cornelison
A journalist hungry for his big break gets the story of a lifetime when a
once-closed rape case resurfaces…and the victim is none other than his
reclusive neighbor. But Jack Calhoun wasn't expecting the onslaught of
attraction for Megan, or the urge to protect her.

SRSCNM0707